Retaliation

Two Worlds Book #4

by Timothy L. Cerepaka

An Annulus Publishing Book

Annulus Publishing, Cherokee, Texas, 2015

Published by Annulus Publishing

Copyright © Timothy L. Cerepaka 2015. All rights reserved.

Formatting by Timothy L. Cerepaka

Contact: timothy@timothylcerepaka.com

Cover design by Elaina Lee of For the Muse Design

(www.forthemusedesign.com)

ISBN-13: 978-0692566541

ISBN-10: 0692566546

Acknowledgments

I would like to thank my uncle, James Wilhite, for helping me get this manuscript into publishable shape. I'd also like to thank the rest of my family for supporting me while I wrote this novel. You guys rock.

Chapter 1

Date: Loday, third day of the week, Gogoth 10th, 3050 XE, 3050 DE

Time: 7:32 PM XST (Xeeon Standard Time), 7:32 AM DST (Delanian Standard Time)

Location: Xeeon, one of the seven city states situated between the Dead Lands and the rest of Xeeo, and the most well-known and populous of them. Population: Three million. Current Mayor is Xacron-Ah, who has reigned over the city for six years. Protected by the J Series Law Enforcement Robots, which were designed and built by Annulus Robotics, Inc.

Objective: Kidnap Mayor Xacron-Ah and take him back to the Foundation's current temporary headquarters for further interrogation.

Status: Power level at 90%.

I stand on the top of one of Xeeon's massive skyscrapers. The sky is quite dark at the moment, but the city itself is alive with lights. Massive telescreens play ads for products such as the new Intelligent Arm Buddy, as well as news reports from the major Xeeonite news stations and even news from Dela. The streets are full of hundreds of people, who despite the time of night appear as lively and awake as ever.

I do not stand in the open, however; instead, I stand behind one of the electronic billboards built directly into the skyscraper's roof. I do this because I am trying to avoid the searching optics and sensors of my fellow J bots, who soar through the sky or stand watch on top of other buildings. There aren't many out at the moment—they probably do not expect any trouble tonight—but I must remain hidden nonetheless. I wish to join them, but I am aware that returning to my fellow officers would cause more harm than good at the moment, especially if they knew what I am about to do.

As for why they have not sensed me yet, that is because Konoa, one of the Foundation's agents, disabled my connections to the Database and my fellow J bots when he repaired me two and a half weeks ago. I cannot activate the communication channels between me and my fellow J bots or between me and the Database even if I want to.

But it is not merely my own tech preventing me from communicating with my fellow J bots. Leaning against the back of the electronic billboard, her arms crossed over her chest, is the female elf known as Lanresia. On the index finger of her right hand, she wears a black skyras ring that is cloaking us from the sensors of my fellow J bots. I know it works because when she tested it on herself back on Dela, I tried to scan for her presence but failed to find her, even though she had only been standing a few feet away from me at the time.

In contrast to my passive demeanor, Lanresia appears restless and afraid. She constantly rubs her skyras ring, every now and then peeking out from around the billboard to see if she can spot

2

RETALIATION

Konoa, although I doubt she can see much with those thick, dark goggles strapped over her eyes. She does not say anything, probably because her speaking snake is deactivated, curled around her waist like a belt, so she cannot speak to me at all.

Not that I am complaining. Our current mission requires as much silence as we are able to create. Speaking is unnecessary; after all, we already spent the past day going over every last detail of the plan. I can recite the entire plan by memory, although I suppose that isn't impressive, seeing as we J bots tend to have picture perfect memory in comparison to organics.

The only reason we have not yet moved from behind the large billboard is because we are awaiting the sign from Konoa. Back on Dela, during the planning stages of this kidnapping, we agreed on a signal for Konoa to give us when it is our turn to move. So far, Konoa has not given us the okay, although I am not disturbed, because we have received no sign so far that Konoa has run into any unexpected problems. He should be giving us the signal any minute now.

As I stand here, I go over the plan in my head, despite having gone over it several times with Lanresia, Konoa, and the Head. Still, we have nothing better to do at the moment, so I feel that it is wise to go over the plan in case there are any problems in it that we somehow missed in the planning stages. Then again, if there are any issues, it is almost certainly too late by now to go back and correct them.

Our ultimate goal is to defeat Reunification, that secretive organization which has the goal of 'reuniting' Dela and Xeeo. In order to learn more about how Reunification is progressing in their goal—which we know very little of due to having no spies within the organization to relay their plans to us—we have decided to kidnap the most well-known and high-profile member of Reunification: Mayor Xacron-Ah.

According to the Foundation, Xacron-Ah's primary job, from what they have gathered, is to keep non-members of Reunification from entering the Dead Lands and accidentally discovering Reunification's operations out there. He uses his authority as the Mayor to enforce laws preventing Xeeonite citizens and even foreigners from entering the Dead Lands.

Therefore, we believe that Xacron-Ah will be able to tell us quite a bit about Reunification. He has been seen in contact with the Leader of Reunification, a woman called Kiriah, which is a good sign that he will be able to offer us valuable intelligence if we can get him.

Our plan, then, is to break into the Mayor's Mansion—a building only a block away from our current position—kidnap Xacron-Ah, and then take him to our current base of operations, where we will then interrogate him for the information we need.

As for how we plan to do that, it is simple. Konoa will start a riot in the streets of Xeeon, which will force the majority of the J bots in the vicinity to try to contain it. While they are distracted by the rioting, Lanresia and I will go to the Mayor's Mansion and break through its security forces, kidnap Xacron-Ah himself, and then leave, hopefully before my fellow officers succeed in ending the riot and returning to check on the Mayor.

In fact, the whole reason I am even here is because I have detailed knowledge of the Mayor's Mansion. I have never served on Xacron-Ah's personal security force; however, the mobile Database stored in my memory contains a map of the Mayor's

Mansion, as well as knowledge of the other security measures put in place to keep him safe. By using my knowledge, we should have little trouble breaking into the Mansion and kidnapping Xacron-Ah, assuming nothing goes wrong.

Even though I understand that this is all for the greater good, my programming makes me want to rebel against it. Defending Xacron-Ah's life is one of the few specific commands directly coded into our AI. We are not supposed to kidnap or hurt him in any way, because he is the Mayor, and the Mayor is considered an even higher authority than the Database among us J bots.

Furthermore, I find the idea of intentionally starting a riot to be legally questionable. As a J bot, it is my duty to stop or prevent riots from breaking out, not to be an accomplice to one. Under ordinary circumstances, I should arrest Konoa and Lanresia both and put them in the Xeeon City Prison, where they will await their trial in the courts.

But right now, I must put aside the law in order to protect it. Even I understand that it is more important to stop Reunification than it is to enforce the law. Besides, if I return to my fellow officers, I will likely be scrapped, as I was framed for the murders of several Knights, which makes me a liability for the J bots as a whole.

Yet when I look at the roof of the Mayor's Mansion—which peeks out over one of the nearby buildings—I find it hard to resist my programming, which tells me to defend the building from those who want to kidnap him. It is a strong ... not exactly a feeling, because we J bots do not have 'feelings' of any sort. It is a command, one that I find difficult to ignore, though I manage it nonetheless.

Lanresia, on the other hand, does not seem to be suffering from the internal strife I am. She only appears worried because she is afraid of my former fellow officers finding and arresting us. She has not told me that, but I can tell, because they are currently the only real threat to our plan.

I have no words of comfort for her, seeing as I do not know how to comfort someone. I consider telling another joke from *Secrets of Humor*, but then decide that it is better to keep silent and not accidentally draw the attention of the law enforcers to us with a joke that she will probably not even laugh at. That is the reason, as far as I can tell, why the Foundation agents I have met do not find my humor appealing; it is Xeeonite humor and they are Delanians, which means that their sense of humor is different from mine, although that does not help me find out exactly what they find humorous and what they don't.

Lanresia, peering around the side of the billboard again, suddenly gestures for me to look around with her. As silently as I can, I walk over to her side and peer around the billboard, though at first I do not understand what she wants me to look at.

Then I see Konoa standing on top of a parked hover vehicle. He is wearing a looser, hood-like skull mask to hide his identity, along with a pair of dark goggles over the eye holes, which I consider unnecessary because his face is not in the Database. Then again, I suppose Konoa probably wishes to stay out of the Database as much as he can, so wearing a mask to hide his identity makes sense.

None of the Xeeonians in the streets appear to take notice of him at first, likely because he has not drawn attention to himself yet, although a handful of human teenagers point and snicker at his mask (they probably think it looks ridiculous). Even my fellow J bots do not stop to demand he show his ID, although that may be because he is not behaving in any illegal manner yet.

Then Konoa raises a large, round object in his hand: a blind bomb. I recall Konoa saying that he is going to use a blind bomb to start the confusion, so I am not surprised to see it. I do wonder where he found such a large one, however, considering most blind bombs are only large enough to fit inside the average human fist.

Lanresia's speaking snake uncurls from around her waist and rises up by her head. Its glowing eyes are looking at Konoa as it says, "Ready, J997?"

I nod and whisper, "Affirmative."

"All right," says Lanresia, her voice as low as mine. "I am going to send Konoa a message telling him to throw the blind bomb now. Just be ready to run for the Mansion as soon as it goes off."

"I am always ready," I say. "And do not worry about getting past Xacron-Ah's security systems; I will handle that when we get there."

"Good," says Lanresia. "Now I am sending this message to Konoa. Once he gets it, he will—"

Lanresia is interrupted when Konoa hefts the large blind bomb and tosses it directly into the center of the loud, busy streets of Xeeon. As soon as the blind bomb lands in the streets, it explodes, creating a massive blinding light that is immediately followed by the terrified and confused screams of the people.

I, however, am not blinded by the light, because I activate the darkening filters on my optics to prevent the blind bomb from damaging them. This allows me to see the J bots soaring from all around the nearby skyscrapers, trying to restore peace and order to the now confused mass of citizens running around and screaming in the streets below. I spot Konoa making a break for it, going in the opposite direction of the Mayor's Mansion, causing several officers to fly after him immediately. Smart move. It means my former fellow officers will be less likely to notice Lanresia and I as we make our way to the Mayor's Mansion.

Lanresia grabs onto my shoulders and I fly us both down to the alleyway between the building we stood on and the one next to it. As we touch the streets, I find it hard to ignore the screams and sounds of rioting in the streets behind us, but I focus my attention solely on our mission, which will matter more in the long run than stopping this riot.

Once Lanresia lets go of my shoulders, the two of us run down the alley, which is completely abandoned. There are not even any beggars here, which is good, because the fewer people who see us, the better.

In less than a minute, we arrive at the area behind the Mayor's Mansion. It is a large building—not quite as large as the skyscrapers that tower it, but large enough—that looks antiquated compared to the rest of the city, which makes sense, seeing as the Mayor's Mansion is older than the rest of Xeeon, having been built by the first settlers of this region fifty years ago or so. Removing my darkening filter (which is no longer necessary, thanks to the light from the blind bomb having gone away) allows me to see that the Mansion has a large dome rising from the center, while four turrets rise from every corner.

The Mayor's Mansion is surrounded by an electric fence on all sides. The electric fence is strong enough to knock out anyone who tries to touch it and can shorten out any electrical gadgets used on it. Even we J bots are not entirely immune from its effects, which is why I am careful to keep my distance.

I see none of my fellow J bots around, but Lanresia and I keep to the shadows anyway. The Mayor's Mansion has security cameras affixed to the outside, which means that it is impossible to enter without being seen. Even simply walking by the Mansion's fence unseen is impossible, because the security cameras are always on and constantly filming everyone and everything that comes near the Mansion's vicinity. If the cameras see us as we try to break into the Mansion, they will send an automated alert to Database to send officers to arrest us, and our entire plan will fall apart.

Other security hazards include motion sensors in the garden around the Mansion, as well as an electric grid running underneath the ground to electrocute any trespassers who somehow make it past the fence. It is quite the well-defended area.

But we are not going to climb or even fly over the fence. That will be too obvious and will ruin the plan before it even passes phase one.

Instead, I bend over and remove the manhole cover on the street near us. Lanresia wrinkles her nose when she looks down it, likely smelling the waste below (which I am unable to, as J bots are not designed with noses or the ability to smell anything). Still, she climbs down the ladder anyway, and I follow suit, pulling the cover over our heads as soon as we are both inside.

We are going down into the sewers because the Mayor's

Mansion has a secret escape route connected to them. No one knows about this secret escape route outside of the Mayor himself and us J bots; in fact, even many of us J bots are ignorant of its existence. I only know of it because I was once chosen to protect the Mayor and given this information, but then it was decided that someone else would do a better job as a bodyguard than I would. I was allowed to keep the information in case of an emergency, although I am not quite sure that this is what the Database was thinking of when it told me that.

The files state that this secret escape route is only to be used if Xeeon is under attack and it is unsafe for the Mayor to escape above ground. If the Mansion's teleporters are broken, the secret escape route leads to a teleporter that will take the Mayor out of Xeeon and to wherever he needs to go in order to be safe.

Lanresia reaches the bottom first. A couple of seconds later, I am standing by her and using my built-in night vision to look at our surroundings.

I have only been down in the sewers of Xeeon a handful of times, so I am not as familiar with their layout as I should have been. They are dark, with dirty water and waste flowing down the center from wherever they come from. I see turned-off lights on the walls, but I have no way to activate them. Lanresia and I stand on the raised edges of the sewers, which appear to go down quite a ways, although the exact length is irrelevant to the plan, so I don't think about it.

Lanresia looks quite sick, because her face is turning green and she has her hands over her stomach. Still, she is not complaining, although I wonder if her sickness might harm us. I hope not, but it is too late to send her back now and I do not have any medicine to help calm her stomach.

According to the mobile Database, we need to walk straight ahead. I lead this time, because I am the only one of us who has an idea of what to expect ahead. Lanresia follows me, but she is so light on her feet that even my advanced audio receptors do not always pick up the sounds of her footsteps.

I walk forward without any reservation, despite the darkness of the sewers. I do this because I know that the secret escape route has no security in it at all—no cameras, no J bots, nothing; this is due to its secrecy. Because no one knows about it, the Mayor thought it is unnecessary to add extra security measures. That is why it will be easy for Lanresia and me to use this route. Assuming all goes well, we should have the Mayor out of here with little trouble.

"J997?" says Lanresia behind me, her voice a whisper. "Did you hear that?"

I stop and look over my shoulder at Lanresia. Her pointed elvish ears are twitching, a sign that she is trying to hone in on a particular sound that she hears. Her facial expression is still quite sick, although she looks like she is trying to concentrate hard on whatever it is she is listening for.

"Hear what, Lanresia?" I ask. "My audio receptors do not pick up anything down here."

Lanresia frowns. "It sounded like claws scraping against brick. And … something swimming in the waste water."

I increase the volume of my audio receptors to see if I can hear that same sound. My audio receptors pick up nothing at first, but then I hear something swimming in the dirty water flowing through the center of the sewers. I peer at the water, but it is so thick with waste that I cannot see through it at all.

"What is it?" Lanresia asks, her voice more than a little worried.

"I cannot see it," I say. "It may simply be a sewer dweller, which is a type of lizard that exists in the sewers of Xeeon and other cities. They are usually harmless, content to swim in the dirty water and waste that flows down here, and do not care to attack anything that does not pose an immediate threat to them."

Lanresia sighs. "Oh, that's good. I thought it might be something worse."

"We have nothing to fear down here," I say, shaking my head and turning away from the waste water. "Nothing at all. The sewers are abandoned even by the city's homeless. No one ever comes down here, aside from sewage workers and maintenance crews, so I believe we will be just fine. We must continue going forward until we find the secret entrance to the Mayor's Mansion."

Lanresia nods, but then she looks at the wall to our right and jumps. "What is that?"

I look at what she has seen. The wall at first looks as slimy and greenish as the rest of the tunnel does, but upon further inspection, I see a dried coating of blood on the wall. Sensors indicate that it is human blood, although when I run a sample through the mobile Database, it does not match any known Xeeonian citizen's blood. This is probably due to the blood's age, as well as the bacteria of the sewer that has no doubt mixed with it.

But it is not just a little blood; it is a lot of blood. It is almost like a second coat of paint. That is indeed strange, but when I look around, I do not see any bodies that the blood could have come from, which makes me wonder where it came from.

"Why is there blood on the wall?" asks Lanresia. She looks like she wants to run, but to her credit, she does not. "What is going on down here?"

"I do not know for certain," I say. "There should not be any blood down here at all. To my knowledge, the only organic beings to have ever been down here were the original workers who built this sewer, but the Database does not record any of them dying."

"I don't like this," says Lanresia. "Let's just hurry on and find the—"

Lanresia is interrupted by the sound of water splashing behind us. I whirl around in time to see a large, humanoid-like lizard creature bursting from the waste water, its open maw revealing row upon row of deadly teeth, its sharp claws extended out before it.

Before I can react, the lizard humanoid grabs me and pulls me back into the waste water with it. I hear Lanresia scream behind me as that happens, but I am unable to respond and her scream is cut off the moment my head goes beneath the surface of the water.

In the waste water, I am unable to see anything due to the thick sewage and waste in my optics. Sensors indicate, however, that the lizard humanoid—which must be one of the same creatures that attacked the Foundation's Delanian and Xeeonite branches two and a half weeks ago—is holding me tight and biting at every part of my body it can reach.

I try to fight back by punching and kicking at the creature, but

13

my body is not designed to fight underwater; therefore, my attacks are weak and ineffective. The lizard humanoid, however, must have been designed to fight here, because it has no trouble at all attacking me through the thick sludge and waste all around us.

Its attacks do not hurt, but I doubt it will be long before it tears through my armor and succeeds in damaging my internals. Therefore, I must end this fight quickly and reunite with Lanresia; although my resolve to end this fight quickly does not make the lizard humanoid fight any less viciously.

But then I remember my electrical barrier, which, if I choose to activate it, will electrocute the lizard humanoid and probably kill it. But I hesitate to do us underwater, because it might end up short-circuiting me as well.

Instead, I activate my laser vision, firing twin beams at the lizard humanoid biting at me. My lasers strike it in the neck, causing the lizard humanoid to let go of me in response. I then kick at it as hard as I can, making contact with its chest, and then activate my boosters to allow me to rocket out of the water quickly.

Bursting through the surface of the waste water, I almost fly into the low ceiling of the escape tunnel before I succeed in stopping myself. Then I hear Lanresia's cry and look to my right to see what is happening to her.

She is surrounded on both sides by a couple of lizard humanoids, although the creatures are keeping their distance from her because she is firing her laser gun at them. She does not hit them, probably because her fear is affecting her aim, but so far she does not appear wounded by them, which is good.

I aim my eye lasers at them, but before I can fire, there is a splash below and the lizard humanoid I fought in the waste water bursts out and grabs onto my ankles. The sudden change in weight throws off my balance and almost causes me to be dragged down back into the water.

But then I put more power into my boosters, sending out large flames that burn the lizard humanoid's hands. It roars in pain and lets go, falling back into the water with a splash, while I regain my balance and look at Lanresia's situation again.

She fires her laser gun at the lizard humanoids, but her aim is poor, likely due to her fear and the darkness overriding her rational senses. The lizard humanoids have no trouble dodging her blasts and are about to attack her, prompting me to fly down toward her as fast as I can.

I land on the concrete floor and then lash out with a kick aimed at one of the lizard humanoids. My foot connects with its jaw, sending it staggering backward from the impact, and then I follow it up with a laser blast from my eyes, striking it in the heart. My lasers cut a black, bloody hole in its chest, causing the lizard humanoid to collapse onto the floor instantly.

Then I turn my attention to the second one, which is standing back as if to analyze me. Lanresia, who is behind me, points her laser gun at it, but before she can pull the trigger and shoot, the lizard humanoid opens its mouth and unleashes a stream of fire at us.

I knock Lanresia down and then step forward to take the brunt of the blast. The flames bathe over me, but I do not feel the heat. However, my internal thermometer says that my temperature is rapidly rising, even with my external cooling shields activating to prevent my exterior from being melted. Even so, the flames are hot enough that I know I must end this quickly before they break through my cooling shields and cause serious damage to my exterior.

The flames obscure my optics, but I can easily guess where the lizard humanoid is. I fire twin lasers at it, hear the lasers sizzle against its skin, and then the flames abruptly cut off. At the same time, my exterior temperature rapidly returns to normal, while the lizard humanoid that had been trying to kill me falls dead on the floor. My lasers appear to have gone through its open mouth, which likely means that they hit its brain.

In any case, these two lizard humanoids are dead, but I still sense the third one in the waste water below. I hesitate to go after it, however, because I know how deadly that creature can fight in the water.

Just as I think that, the lizard humanoid splashes out from the water again, roaring like a Great Lizard as it lunges toward me. Without hesitation, I raise my hand and fire a single finger lightning bolt at the creature.

The finger lightning bolt strikes it in the chest, causing it to roar in pain as it is electrocuted. It falls back into the water, splashing up more waste as it does so, but this time, my sensors pick up no signs of life below. That final lightning bolt likely did the trick.

I turn to Lanresia. She is panting hard and looking sicker and more frightened than ever, even though all signs indicate that we are currently safe from any other unexpected threats.

"Those monsters are down here?" says Lanresia, still holding her gun as if the battle is not over. "You said that there weren't any guards down here. Why—"

16

"I admit to being wrong about that, but the explanation is quite logical," I say. "The lizard humanoids work for Reunification. Most likely, Xacron-Ah placed them down here in order to more effectively protect himself from possible intruders. I doubt he thought anyone would actually come this way, but he obviously wanted to be safer than sorry."

Lanresia's eyes flick to the blood-stained wall. "What about the blood, then?"

"I do not know," I say. "Perhaps someone else came down here—likely a sewer worker, seeing as this is still part of the sewers and no one else knows about this place—and the lizard humanoids attacked and killed him under the mistaken belief that he was a threat to Xacron-Ah's life."

As I say that, a hat floats by us on the waste water. It appears to me to be the cap usually worn by Xeeon sewer workers, although it is so covered in grime and waste that I cannot tell for sure.

Lanresia shivers. "Those things are so horrible. Just awful."

I nod. "They are indeed quite terrifying, but there is no reason for us to be afraid. They are all dead, and it is unlikely that there are any more down here, because I doubt Xacron-Ah thought he needed more than that."

Lanresia holds her gun close to her chest, however. "Maybe, but I'm going to keep my gun out anyway."

Because I do not expect us to get into any more fights, I find her desire to keep her gun un-holstered rather odd.

I am about to comment on it before I remember that Lanresia has already had terrible experiences with these creatures. She is one of the few survivors of Reunification's assault on the

Foundation's Xeeonite branch and is also a survivor of Reunification's attack on the Foundation's Delanian branch. She may even be suffering from some kind of stress disorder, although I again say nothing about it, because aside from this odd (yet understandable) action of hers, she seems to be functioning as normally as ever. Still, I resolve to keep a closer eye on her in case the stress of the situation causes her to break down, however unlikely that may seem at the moment.

With the lizard humanoids out of the way, it only takes us a few more minutes of walking to find the secret ladder leading up to the Mayor's Mansion. The ladder is hidden behind a portion of the concrete wall that resembles every other part of the wall; however, my keen optics spy a cracked part of the wall which resembles a panel. I press my hand against it and the wall slides away, revealing a rather simple metal ladder leading up into the shadows above.

This time, I go first, because I am better able to handle whatever may await us above than Lanresia is. I doubt we will run into any real problems, however, because this ladder should take us directly to Xacron-Ah's bedroom. Knowing the Mayor's schedule, he should be either asleep or about to go to sleep at this very moment. Xacron-Ah always sleeps alone in his room, so we probably will not run into any guards. Of course, he usually has his bodyguards stationed outside his room, so Lanresia and I will need to be as silent as the Dead Lands once we get there.

It takes us only a couple of minutes of climbing to reach the hatch leading into Xacron-Ah's room. The hatch is normally locked, but I know the secret combination to undo it.

Unfortunately, the hatch is locked from the outside. It is

designed to allow someone to *leave* Xacron-Ah's room, not enter it via the sewers. That is why it cannot be unlocked from the inside.

Even this problem is not as insurmountable as it first appears, however. A quick but careful application of my laser vision destroys the lock and allows me to lift it.

But I do not throw the hatch open; instead, I carefully raise it inch by inch. While I doubt Xacron-Ah will notice, seeing as this hatch is carefully hidden in his room, I cannot risk him noticing us before he needs to.

As I lift the hatch, I gradually gain a better view of the room it is in. It is a dark room, not very large, without any lights or any furniture in it. There is a door directly in front of us, however, which should lead us into his closet, which will then lead us into his actual room.

Seeing no one here, I lift the hatch all the way open and climb out. Lanresia follows me and looks happy that we are no longer down there. She still does not holster her gun, however, and when she looks at me, she wrinkles her nose again.

"You smell awful," says Lanresia in a whisper. "Must be the sewage water."

"I do not think it matters," I say. "I can still kidnap Xacron-Ah whether I smell good or bad."

"What if he smells you before we sneak up on him?" says Lanresia. She pinches her nose. "Because when I say you smell awful, I mean *awful.*"

"I have no way of cleaning myself off," I say. "But I wonder if your concealment ring can also hide scents."

Lanresia glances at the skyras ring on her finger and says, "I think so, but that requires more skyras usage than normal. I may not be able to maintain it for long."

"You do not need to," I say. "All you need to do is maintain it for a few minutes. That is all the time we will need to kidnap Xacron-Ah."

"If you say so," says Lanresia. "You seem pretty confident about our ability to kidnap him."

"I know neither confidence nor doubt," I say. "As a robot, I know only that I must do what I must do."

"Right," says Lanresia, who has a hint of doubt in her voice. "Well, let's just get going. There's no telling how much time we have before the J bots get that crowd under control and return to their original positions, which will make it harder for us to escape with Xacron-Ah once we catch him."

I nod and walk over to the door in front of us. It is unlocked, allowing me to wave my hand and cause the door to slide open. I find that odd, because I expected it to be locked. Then again, if Xacron-Ah ever needs to make a quick escape, it is probably more practical for him to keep this door unlocked than locked.

When Lanresia and I step through the doorway, we find ourselves hidden behind rows of large suits, equally-large shirts, and other clothing. The mobile Database says that Xacron-Ah's secret escape route is hidden within his closet, which explains the presence of so many suits hanging in front of us.

Based on the darkness of the closet, the door must be closed; however, when I push aside some of the suits (thus getting some of the waste water on them, although that is unimportant at the moment), I see that the closet door is in fact cracked open just slightly. It appears that Xacron-Ah has failed to close the door for some reason. Then again, I recall that Xacron-Ah is well-known for his sloppiness in minor matters such as this, so this is not surprising.

Still, Lanresia and I push aside his suits as quietly as we can. I do not know if Xacron-Ah is in fact in his room yet or if he is even awake. All I know is that we must be careful nonetheless; this entire plan hinges on our kidnapping Xacron-Ah. If we fail now, it is highly unlikely we will get an opportunity to try this again.

As it turns out, however, Xacron-Ah's closet has more than merely clothes in it. We step over old, forgotten pairs of shoes, cardboard boxes containing objects we cannot see, and other articles of clothing, such as ties and socks. Once we even find a tiny metal ball that hums when you touch it, but thankfully we learn how to turn it off and do so before it can alert Xacron-Ah's attention to his closet.

As we walk closer to the door, I see blue lights flashing through the crack, as well as voices that sound like they are deep in conversation. One of them is Xacron-Ah's deep, rumbling voice; the other is unfamiliar, although if Xacron-Ah's tone is a clue, he is clearly someone with authority over the Mayor.

Enhancing my audio receptors, I listen hard to Xacron-Ah's conversation, gesturing at Lanresia to stop so I can hear him more clearly.

"... yes, Founder, of course," says Xacron-Ah. He sounds worn out, but he is clearly making an effort to hide it. "No, we have had no luck in locating that rogue J bot on Dela. I've been working with Kalcan to find him, but Kalcan says that he can't find him anywhere. On the plus side, we've moved more shipments of super speed from Dela to Xeeo in the past couple of days than we did in all of last month."

I look at Lanresia, who is now staring at me in surprise. It is obvious to us both that Xacron-Ah is talking about me, unless there happens to be another 'rogue' J bot somewhere on Dela who is also working against Reunification.

Even more interesting, however, is his reference to someone with the title 'Founder.' That title can only belong to the mysterious and enigmatic head of Reunification, which means that Xacron-Ah is speaking with him right now; if so, then I may be able to get my first glimpse of the Founder if I am careful.

Gesturing for Lanresia to stay still, I make my way to the cracked door, still listening to the conversation all the while.

"You better find him quick," says the unfamiliar voice, which I believe belongs to the Founder. "I do not like having someone outside of our organization knowing about us and our plans, even if we have discredited his witness by framing him for the murder of those Knights. And I do not care about the drugs, despite the role they will play in the completion of the Mission."

"Yes, Founder, I understand," says Xacron-Ah. "But don't worry. If that J bot ever steps back on Xeeo and tries to reconnect with the Database, I will be the first to know, and he will be reprogrammed and his memory wiped entirely, if not scrapped outright."

That does not alarm me, mostly because my lack of emotion makes it hard for me to feel alarmed at anything. Nonetheless, I hear the sincerity in Xacron-Ah's voice, which tells me he fully intends on carrying out that promise should he ever get his hands on me.

RETALIATION

Reaching the door, I peer through the crack as carefully as I can, adjusting my optics to see better in the darkness of Xacron-Ah's room.

Due to the thinness of the crack, I cannot see much; however, I can see Xacron-Ah's massive back to me. He appears to be wearing his navy blue suit; unusual, seeing as he is by himself. Then again, it is highly likely that Xacron-Ah is wearing his suit because he just returned from an important political meeting of some sort. Seeing as I do not have access to his personal calendar, I cannot tell for sure.

Due to Xacron-Ah's bulk, it is hard for me to see the Founder, who appears to be a glowing blue hologram projecting in front of Xacron-Ah. I catch a glimpse of a head that appears half-organic, half-mechanical, which is unusual; however, I see nothing else besides that.

"I hope so," says the Founder. "It would not be good for us if this robot allied with the remnants of the Foundation. I am not afraid of a simple machine; however, I do worry about the Foundation, who have proven themselves time and again to be a thorn in our side."

"You don't need to worry about anything, Founder," says Xacron-Ah. "The Foundation is gone. Its twin bases on Xeeo and Dela are destroyed, most of its members are dead, and those few who survived both assaults are scattered and on the run, unable to do anything except try to survive. I even succeeded in having my J bots arrest a few of them, including Kojama himself not more than a few hours ago."

A tiny, slightly metallic gasp behind me makes me look over my shoulder at Lanresia's speaking snake. Lanresia is standing

23

near me, having somehow moved close to me without me noticing. She looks shocked and terrified, which puzzles me, as I do not know who this 'Kojama' fellow is. She does, apparently, but I decide to ask her more about him later.

"Kojama?" says the Founder. "Interesting. When will you execute him?"

"His execution is scheduled for the morning," says Xacron-Ah, who sounds proud of himself. "Remember the Jaws massacre that happened a few weeks back?"

"I recollect you telling me about that sometime ago," says the Founder. "Was not that the regretful day when a mad man entered the area of Xeeon known as 'the Jaws' and killed ten Rathonian immigrants, including three children?"

"Yes," says Xacron-Ah, nodding his large head, making his dreads fly about. "The J bots did not arrive in time to stop him. The killer is still on the loose; however, I am blaming Kojama for the murders that shocked the city. Since no one knows what the killer's face actually looks like, no one is questioning whether he is indeed the killer or not. We have fabricated evidence to fool the media into believing that he is the culprit, which they've eaten up like cake. About the only thing we've done is make sure that the media doesn't have any picture of him or his name."

"Why?" says the Founder.

"Our excuse is that we don't want to make a killer famous and thus inspire other killers like him to perform a repeat of the Jaws massacres in order to get that same level of fame," says Xacron-Ah, who sounds quite proud of himself. "But I'm sure you know the real reasons why I'm doing it."

"Of course," says the Founder. "A wise move all around. You

24

not only will kill one of the Foundation's most important members, but you will also do it without alerting the public to either organization's existence. Well done, Xacron-Ah, well done."

"All for the Mission, Founder," says Xacron-Ah. "I believe as you do, that anyone who stands in our way must die."

"That is the truest statement you have made in a long time," says the Founder. "Now I must let you know that we are closer than ever to completing the Mission. Indeed, I speculate it will only take us a few more days to do so, due to our rapid progress."

"Wonderful to hear, Found—" says Xacron-Ah, before the Founder interrupts him.

"Which is why I am speaking with you so early in the morning," says the Founder. His tone becomes harsher. "With the Mission so close to completion at this point, we cannot afford even the smallest of mistakes from any of our agents, including you. Do you hear me?"

Xacron-Ah steps back, even though the Founder is merely a hologram that cannot hurt him. "Why, er, yes, Founder, I understand completely. I have done my best in everything that I do. I would never make a mistake that could cost us the entire Mission."

"I know how eagerly you believe that," says the Founder. "But I must repeat it: *Do not make any mistakes.* If you slip up even once, when we are so close to healing the worlds, I will know about it, and you will not live long enough to repeat it, much less regret it."

Xacron-Ah runs his hand through his locks. "Yes, sir, I understa—"

"You are not important," the Founder interrupts again.

"Remember that your life is insignificant in the long run. You are not so important that I will hesitate to snuff out your insignificant life if you make a mistake. Every step you take, you take on the narrow road, with death awaiting to embrace you on either side of the deep, dark pit you walk over."

"Yes, sir, of cou—"

"Good," says the Founder. "Now I believe we have covered everything. I must now go and return to my chambers. As for you, make no mistakes, do not attract any unnecessary attention to yourself, and use whatever force necessary to subdue our enemies."

Xacron-Ah bows deeply, allowing me a glimpse of the holographic Founder. He wears golden wizard robes and has a half-organic, half-mechanical face. Not entirely unusual, seeing as many Xeeonites have 'two-faces,' as the slang for those types of faces goes, but the Founder's face does not look like a typical two-face.

Then Xacron-Ah rises to his full height again and the Founder is gone from my view once more. "Yes, Founder, sir. I understand. Glory be to the Mission!"

"Indeed," says the Founder. "If anything comes up, contact Kiriah immediately. At this point, I cannot be distracted by anything less than the most urgent of emergencies. Understood?"

"Yes, Founder sir," says Xacron-Ah. "I will make certain of it."

"Very well," says the Founder. "Assuming all goes well within the next day or so, the next time we see each other, it will be on the healed world, where all is one."

Then the Founder's hologram vanishes. As soon as it does,

Xacron-Ah gasps and staggers back. He puts a hand on his forehead, but with his back to us, I cannot see his face. However, my sensors indicate that his blood pressure is rising fast.

"Oh god," says Xacron-Ah, panting as though he has run a mile. "Oh god, oh god, how did I get into this? Why, why, why."

His sudden fear cause me to look at Lanresia. She, however, appears to be thinking too deeply about this 'Kojama' person, whoever he is, to notice Xacron-Ah's odd behavior.

I turn my attention to the crack in the door, watching as Xacron-Ah begins pacing back and forth across his room, disappearing and reappearing in my view every now and then.

"This is deeper than I've ever thought I'd be in," says Xacron-Ah. He appears to be talking to himself. "I was promised riches and fame and I got that, but god does that man scare me. I'm not even sure he's a man. Just what the hell is he, anyway? Some kind of immortal monster, that's what he is."

He appears to be talking about the Founder, which puzzles me. He must not be as loyal to the Founder or to Reunification as he appears.

Xacron-Ah stops and begins pulling at his locks, which I recognize as one of his nervous habits, according to the mobile Database's files on him. "Thinks he can boss me around and threaten me. *Me*, Xacron-Ah, Mayor of Xeeon, best former super speed dealer in the world. And then he just blows off the good news about how our shipments are coming along, even though he *told* me to increase productivity. What the hell. Who does he think he is?"

Lanresia moves a little bit closer to the door. She seems to be listening to Xacron-Ah's rambling as well.

27

Then Xacron-Ah falls to his knees and hides his face in his hands. "Oh god, what if he heard me say that? Of course, he probably didn't. My communicator is off and the room isn't bugged. I made sure of that. No, he can't hear me. Bastard can't hear me at all. Unless he's got some weird magic, but—"

Abruptly, Xacron-Ah is up and pacing again. "About the only good thing that idiot's done for me is help me win this office. Even then, being Mayor isn't all that great. Endless meetings, political scheming among the members of Parliament, stupid people demanding I support this or that law, having to pretend that I give a damn about the people who live in this awful city … sometimes, I think this is a horrible nightmare that will end if I would only just wake the *hell* up."

It appears to me that Xacron-Ah must have some kind of mental condition. Possibly the stress of the job is getting to him, although I do not recall ever hearing from the others about this side of the Mayor. His mobile Database files do not mention him being diagnosed with any sort of mental illness, though perhaps he has never seen a psychiatrist about it.

Then Xacron-Ah stops and stomps his foot without warning. "Just brushing off my good report about the drugs … doesn't he realize that this wouldn't be possible if I wasn't in charge of the city? He's the one who harped on and on and on and *on* to me about the importance of these drugs in distracting the J bots and the general population from the Mission, but now he's acting like it's as trivial as a child's toy? What an idiot."

Now that is a particular piece of information I had not known. It is true that smuggling and usage of super speed drugs among the population of Xeeon and its surrounding countryside and cities has increased tenfold ever since Xacron-Ah's election to the position of Mayor of Xeeon; however, I did not know that it is because of Xacron-Ah's aid. That certainly explains why Reunification hired a former drug dealer to lead the city.

"I can't handle this," says Xacron-Ah. He licks his lips and looks at something over his shoulder, out of sight. "I need my hit. I need it. Gotta calm down. Can't sleep if I'm worried about everything. Nope. Can't."

He walks out of my line of sight. Then I hear a drawer open, followed by it closing again. Next, I hear Xacron-Ah sitting down on what sounds like a chair and then a low moan of pleasure that I have little trouble recognizing as the moan of an individual who is injecting super speed into his body.

I look at Lanresia. Her hands cover her mouth; her organic mouth, that is. Her speaking snake's mouth is unobstructed.

"Think we should get him now?" says Lanresia, her voice a low whisper, although thanks to my enhanced audio receptors, I still hear her well.

"Wait," I whisper in return, holding up one hand. "Just wait. Let us wait until Xacron-Ah is too drugged to fight back."

Lanresia frowns, but nods. "Okay."

Of course, I do not know how long it will take for Xacron-Ah to do so. Depending on how used his body is to the drug, he might take anywhere from five minutes to several hours before he is knocked out by the drugs. His fatigue should help, however, because it is a well-known fact about super speed that the amount a person uses directly correlates with how tired they feel now.

We stand in his closet, listening closely to Xacron-Ah's moans of pleasure. He seems to have a high tolerance for the drug, because he still sounds like he is aware. This does not surprise me, however, because due to his past as a dealer of the drug, Xacron-Ah's body likely has developed a tolerance for the drug, despite its destructive effects on the human body. Again, the mobile Database does not mention Xacron-Ah having a history of drug usage, but at this point, I expected that, as the mobile Database does not seem to have any useful information on anything anymore.

Then—without warning—a loud *thump* breaks the monotony. Lanresia and I continue to stand here, however, and listen for a couple of more minutes for Xacron-Ah to continue moaning; instead, we hear him snoring loudly.

With a nod at Lanresia, I quickly but carefully push open the closet door. It opens softly against the carpeted floor, making virtually no noise. Once it is open completely, Lanresia and I step into Xacron-Ah's room.

This is the first time I have stepped foot in this place, because we J bots—even Xacron-Ah's bodyguards—are not allowed in here. Therefore, I look around at the room in order to commit it to my memory.

It is a large, wide-open room, almost taking up the entire floor that it is on. The floor has soft elfish carpeting, while the walls have fine oak wood paneling. An entertainment center, with a large black sofa and a hologram projector, takes up the center of the room, while the door to the bathroom is opened slightly on the other side of the room.

Xacron-Ah's bed is about a dozen feet away from us. It is a large bed, appropriate for a man of his size, with red drapes surrounding it. It looks more Delanian than Xeeonite, which makes sense, seeing as Xacron-Ah is a native of Dela and not Xeeo.

But Xacron-Ah is not sleeping on his bed. The Mayor is instead lying on the floor next to his bed, snoring loudly, his arms splayed out. In his right hand is a needle full of the green liquid known as super speed, although 'full' is not the most correct word. It is half-full at best, although that is still far too much super speed for one human to inject into himself.

In front of Xacron-Ah is a chest of drawers. The top drawer is open, which is no doubt where he kept the needle. I consider digging around inside it to find out what else Xacron-Ah is hiding from us, but then I remember that we have very little time as is and that we need to spend most of that time dragging Xacron-Ah out of here.

Lanresia and I walk up to the unconscious Xacron-Ah, who, aside from his snoring, is not moving at all. I remove the super speed needle from his hand and toss it into the nearest trash can. Then Lanresia and I grab his arms and begin dragging him toward his closet.

Xacron-Ah is a large, heavy man; however, we J bots can lift up to two tons of metal, so dragging him along is not much of a challenge for me. Lanresia, on the other hand, appears to be putting her all into helping. I consider telling her that she does not need to and that I can drag and even carry Xacron-Ah all on my own, but as we are trying to be as quiet as possible, I decide not to mention it.

We have little trouble carrying Xacron-Ah through the open doorway of his closet; however, just to be safe, I close it when we get inside. I doubt anyone will be checking on Xacron-Ah until

31

the morning, by which time we will be long gone; however, I do not want to take any chances.

Kicking aside shoes and other assorted items on the floor of Xacron-Ah's closet, we make our way to the back, where the door to the secret escape route is still open. I find it interesting how close we are to escaping without anyone noticing, but I keep my mouth shut. While I am not superstitious at all, even I have noticed at times how easy it is to 'jinx' oneself, as the Delanians tend to put it.

Considering how important this mission is, I cannot afford to 'jinx' either of us.

When we arrive at the hatch, this is where we meet our first real obstacle. While Xacron-Ah is still sleeping and snoring as soundly as ever, we do not seem to have any easy way to transport Xacron-Ah down it. His bulk should fit through, seeing as the hatch is wide; however, I do not know if I can carry him down myself.

Turning to Lanresia, I ask, "Do you have any idea how we can transport Xacron-Ah down the hatch?"

Lanresia strokes her chin. "We need some sort of platform we could use to lower him down on."

I look around the dark, furniture-less room. "I do not see any platform on hand or even any rope or cables we could use to lower him down with."

Lanresia shrugs. "Then I don't know how we can move him out of here. Unless you think you can hold him over your shoulder while climbing down at the same time?"

I shake my head. "Negative. While I do have the strength necessary to lift up Xacron-Ah, trying to climb down the ladder while supporting him on my shoulder at the same time is impossible."

"I knew it," says Lanresia. She looks at Xacron-Ah in worry. "Then how do we get him out of here? It's not like we can just take the elevator."

I consider the problem logically for a few seconds before a possible solution occurs to me when I glance at the unconscious Xacron-Ah. "I have an idea."

"What is it?" says Lanresia.

"I will show it to you," I say. "Stand back and watch."

Lanresia does as I ask, giving me some room to move. I bend over Xacron-Ah, who is still snoring without end, and shake him gently as I say, in a low voice, "Mayor Xacron-Ah, please wake up. Can you hear me, Mayor Xacron-Ah?"

Lanresia immediately grabs my shoulder. I look over my shoulder at her and see an alarmed look on both of her faces.

"What the hell do you think you're doing?" says Lanresia, her voice still little more than a whisper. "If you wake him up, he'll call in his guards, and the whole plan will be ruined."

"I understand your concerns, Lanresia, but please do not worry," I say, shrugging off her hand. "I know what I am doing. We will not be caught and Xacron-Ah will certainly not call in his bodyguards. Of that, I can assure you."

Lanresia's faces look at me skeptically, but then she steps back and folds her arms across her shoulder. She does not look away, however; instead, she focuses on me with a look that is quite clearly disapproving of my plan, even though she does not yet know what it is.

Turning back to face Xacron-Ah, I gently shake him again,

saying, "Mister Mayor, are you wake?"

Then Xacron-Ah's snoring ceases and his eyes flicker open. He looks at me, but I can already tell that the super speed has destroyed his comprehension. His pupils are smaller and his eyes are bloodshot already, while his breath is unsteady.

"Huh?" says Xacron-Ah, staring at me with blank eyes I recognize from many arrests of super speed dealers. "What are you? Where am I?"

"Mister Mayor, you are on your way to a very important meeting with the Xeeon Parliament," I say. "I am waking you up to get you ready to go. It's starting in ten minutes."

Xacron-Ah makes a dismissive grunt and says, "Bah. Those Parliament idiots can jump into the volcanic pits for all I care. Wake me for something important."

Xacron-Ah tries to close his eyes, but I shake him again, causing him to snap, "What is it now?"

"Sir, you have an important date with Kiriah," I say. "It is in ten minutes and I—"

Xacron-Ah sits up so quickly that he almost knocks his head into mine. He looks around wildly and says, "I have a date with her? Where? What time is it? Am I dressed and ready to go?"

I look at Lanresia, who is staring at me in sheer disbelief.

Then I look at Xacron-Ah and gesture at the hatch behind him. "Sir, we can reach the date quickly if we climb down this hatch into the sewers. It is a short cut to the place you agreed to meet her at."

Xacron-Ah staggers to his feet and almost falls into the hatch headfirst before regaining his balance. He then brushes his locks back and says, "How do I look? Do I look good?"

"Perfect, sir," I say. "Now we must leave soon, because Kiriah is waiting."

"Yes, yes, I agree," says Xacron-Ah, nodding. He pats the lip of the hatch. "Down this hatch, right?"

"Right," I say. I gesture at the ladder. "Just watch your step, because it is a long way down and if you fall on your head, that would force you to push back the date again."

"Again?" says Xacron-Ah, staring at me in alarm. "You mean I've missed my date with her before?"

"Yes," I say with as much sincerity as I can. "Several times, in fact. That is why we must hurry; in fact, that is why you told me to wake you up in time for your date today."

"Of course, of course," says Xacron-Ah. "Thank you so much. I should give you a raise and a promotion for all your hard work."

"It is nothing," I say, ignoring Lanresia's disbelieving stare. "I am only doing what any good servant would do in my situation."

"Very well," says Xacron-Ah. "I'll just climb down this ladder, then."

"I will come with you," I say. "You might not remember the date's location, so I will lead you there."

"Thanks," says Xacron-Ah. "You're a lifesaver. I don't know how I can repay you."

"Again, it is nothing," I say. "Now we must hurry, before Kiriah decides you are not going to show up and leaves."

Xacron-Ah nods and climbs down the ladder far more quickly than a man of his bulk should have been able to. I am about to follow when Lanresia says, "How did you do that?"

I look at Lanresia, who still has her arms folded across her chest. She is looking at me with extreme skepticism, as if I just

35

performed some kind of magic trick that she cannot figure out on her own.

So I say, "One of the effects of super speed over usage is heightened susceptibility. I can effectively make Xacron-Ah do whatever I want simply by suggesting it to him."

Lanresia shakes her head in amazement. "Why didn't I think of that?"

"I've dealt with super speed dealers and users dozens of times before," I say. "It's how I learned about it. Now come on. If we let Xacron-Ah get too far ahead of us, we will lose him."

Chapter 2

Xacron-Ah, in his drug-addled state, is very agreeable up until we emerge from the original secret entrance to the sewers, where we emerge onto the back streets behind his mansion. He takes one look at the back of his mansion, blinks several times, and appears to be coming to his senses when Lanresia knocks him out with a punch to the head.

"I did not know you were so strong, Lanresia," I say as I look down on Xacron-Ah's unconscious body. "I always thought you were quite … well, not exactly weak, but not strong enough to knock a full-grown human male out in one hit."

Lanresia shakes her hand, perhaps because she hurt it when she punched him. "We elves are much stronger than we look. Anyway, pick him up. If someone sees Xacron-Ah lying on the street like this, then we'll have the entire Xeeonite City police force upon us in minutes."

I nod and lift Xacron-Ah's unconscious form over my shoulder. He is quite heavy, but due to my enhanced strength, lifting him is not as difficult as it might have been.

With Lanresia's cloaking ring still protecting us from being seen, the two of us dash off into the alley, ignoring the sounds of the people continuing to riot in the streets.

Thanks to the maps in the mobile Database, we are able to successfully avoid detection from the other J bots and civilians. That is because we take a route that is largely absent of people; in fact, there are not very many homeless people over here, either, a factor I attribute more to luck than anything.

We are in Sector Four, one of Xeeon's six Sectors. This Sector is known for its poverty and homelessness and abandoned property due to the rampant crime that rules this place. We J bots have in the past made attempts to deal with the crime of Sector Four, but the problems underlying this Sector's poverty and crime are too deep for normal crime-fighting methods to work. It does not help that most of the inhabitants of this part of Xeeon do not trust law enforcement of any kind, including us.

That's not the only reason we are trying to return to our headquarters undetected, however. As Xacron-Ah has demonstrated, Reunification has many agents everywhere, and you cannot always tell who they are at first glance. We therefore have to be careful about who sees us and who does not, which we have been very good at doing over the past two and a half weeks.

We arrive at the current 'headquarters' of the Foundation, an old, rundown apartment building that no one lives in anymore and that, to my knowledge, is not owned by anyone, either. The building looks exactly like every other abandoned apartment building in this part of the city, with broken, boarded up windows, chipped front steps, and garbage strewn in front of it. Its windows are grimy and dirt-covered and there is no sign at all that anyone lives in it, or has ever lived in it, for that matter.

Yet its decrepit and abandoned appearance is precisely the point behind our decision to use it as our current base. It decreases the chances of someone stumbling onto us and reporting our presence to the J bots; after all, most people, even the homeless, tend to avoid these abandoned buildings like the plague.

Lanresia and I quickly make our way up the front steps and enter by pulling open the creaky sliding front door. Once we are safely inside, I look around at the entryway. It is a dark, grimy area, with dust and dirt over the floor, holes in the walls, and peeling wallpaper everywhere. The 'WELCOME' rug on the floor is rotted and eaten through, and I have been told by Lanresia and the others that this place has an awful smell as well, somewhere between the stink of super speed and decaying plaster.

In any case, I am glad to be here. Every minute I spend out in the city increases the chances of my former allies finding and arresting me. By being in here, where no J bots ever go, I am at least somewhat safe.

As I kick the dirt off the soles of my feet, Lanresia walks ahead of me, shouting, "Head! We're back! We got Xacron-Ah. Mission successful."

There is no response from the Head; however, someone appears at the top of the stairs and shouts, "You did? Great! Let me see."

The being who runs down the stairs is a Jikorian, one of the major sapient species of Xeeo. While humanoid, there is no mistaking the Jikorian's large forehead or dark green skin for that of a human's. She wears the typical gray uniform that many Foundation agents seem to wear, with a long coat thrown over her shoulders for good measure.

"Hello, Rakam," says Lanresia as the Jikorian jumps down the last few steps and dashes over to us without hesitation. "Any update on Reunification's activities while we were away?"

Rakam, one of the few Foundation agents who survived the massacre on Xeeo's Foundation base, skids to a halt before us and shakes her head. "No. So far, Reunification has been very quiet and impossible to detect with the simple equipment we've got. Anyway, is that really Xacron-Ah?"

I heft the large man who still lies unconscious over my shoulder. "The one and only."

Rakam claps her hands together in excitement. "Oh, I am so happy about this. Looks like our weeks of planning have finally paid off."

"Yes, I agree," says Lanresia. She looks around and frowns. "Where is Konoa? I thought he'd get back here before us."

"We received a message from him a few minutes ago," says Rakam. "He said that he's still trying to shake off the J bots who are tailing him. Said he'll be back before breakfast, though."

Lanresia rubs her hands together. "Oh, I hope he does. If he gets captured ..."

Lanresia does not finish the sentence, but even I understand what she is afraid of happening to her lover. I decide to make a joke to make her feel a little better, as I understand that anxiety can impair performance in organic beings like her.

So I say, "Lanresia, Konoa is going to be all right. It's not like he's running off with a beautiful Rathonian princess, right?"

As I have come to expect from organics, both Lanresia and Rakam look at me as though I am malfunctioning. Clearly, the two do not get the joke.

"It's a joke," I say. "It's based on the story of the son of that rich human Xeeonite businessman, who ran off with a princess of Rathonia to start his own family. Get it?"

The two shake their heads. They still stare at me like I have confused them.

"Never mind," I say. "Looks like I need to continue to work on my delivery, then."

"Uh, right," says Rakam. She peers at Xacron-Ah more closely and a smile appears across her face. "Yes, that is him all right. Let's take him to the basement and tie him up down there. I'll keep an eye on him while you two can go and report the status of your mission to the Head."

Lanresia nods, but then says, "Wait a minute, Rakam. We have something important to report."

"What is it?" asks Rakam. "Did you learn something about Reunification while kidnapping Xacron-Ah?"

"Not exactly," says Lanresia. "But we learned that Kojama survived Reunification's assault on the Xeeonite base and he has been arrested. He's going to be executed later this morning, according to Xacron-Ah."

Rakam's tiny blue eyes widen considerably. "Later this morning? Where?"

"I don't know," says Lanresia, shaking her head. "We overheard Xacron-Ah reporting Kojama's arrest and scheduled execution to the Founder, but he didn't mention all of the details about it, so—"

"We need to break Kojama out of prison, then," says Rakam. "As soon as possible."

Lanresia nods, but then I say, "Excuse me for interrupting, but who, exactly is this Kojama individual and what makes him so important? I recollect Lanresia mentioning him once before sometime ago, but at the time she did not elaborate on who he is."

Rakam and Lanresia look at me again, only this time, it is without the awkward stares from before.

"Oh, that's right," says Rakam, snapping her long nails with a *click*. "You haven't been an agent of the Foundation for very long, so of course you don't know who Kojama is. I'm sorry, I'm just so used to you now that I forgot you are still so new to the Foundation."

Technically, I do not consider myself an agent of the Foundation. While I do work alongside them, it is for the greater good and safety of the Xeeonian people, not because I agree with the organization itself. In truth, I find the Foundation only a little less untrustworthy than Reunification, largely because they still have not shared all of their secrets with me.

Instead of saying all of that, however, I say, "Then tell me who Kojama is and why he is so important."

"We'll tell you after we secure Xacron-Ah," says Rakam. "So why don't we put Xacron-Ah in the basement, like I said earlier, and then go to the Head to report your success? Lanresia can explain Kojama to you better than I, because those two knew each other quite well."

Although I wish to know more about Kojama right away, I see the logic in her suggestion, so I nod and say, "All right. I will go and put Xacron-Ah in the basement right away and make sure that he cannot escape on his own."

After locking up Xacron-Ah in the basement, where we tie him to a chair and gag him with some old rags lying around the place and also remove his com-watch from him so he cannot call for help from the outside world, Lanresia and I head up to the second floor, where the Head lives, while Rakam volunteers to stay at the entrance to the basement in case Xacron-Ah wakes up and tries to escape somehow.

As we climb the steps, Lanresia says to me, "Kojama was one of the best members of the Foundation. He could speak a dozen different languages fluently, had an unmatched understanding of inter-world politics, and was a great robotics mechanic on top of all of that. He even built his own prosthetic legs after losing his organic ones after a terrible accident."

"He sounds like quite the individual," I say.

"He was," says Lanresia with a sigh. "He and I joined the Foundation at the same time, about six years ago, actually. We became friends and worked together on several missions. Konoa was always jealous of our closeness, even though he knows I love him and him alone and only ever thought of Kojama as a friend."

"What species is Kojama, anyway?" I ask when we reach the top of the stairs and turn to the left, down the hallway that will take us to the Head's room. "Human?"

"Part human, part elf," says Lanresia. "He always identified as human, though. I think he was ashamed of his elfish heritage because of elves' natural dislike of Xeeonite technology, while he embraced it, since he was born and raised on this world."

"I see," I say as we walk by door after door down the hall. "What happened to him?"

"That's the thing," says Lanresia. "When those horrible lizard monsters attacked our Xeeonite base, I thought for sure he had died in the initial assault. He didn't come with the survivors to the

43

Delanian base, nor have we been able to find him since the Head began looking for any agents who survived the attacks. That he survived at all, even if he is in the custody of the law and is about to be executed, is great news, because that means he's still alive. And if we can rescue him, he could be of great help to us all."

"He does indeed sound like a great individual," I say. "But it may be too late to save him, if Xacron-Ah is telling the truth about the time of his execution."

"I'm sure the Head will come up with a plan to save him," says Lanresia. "I know the Head greatly respected Kojama and knew how useful he was, because she always gave him the most important missions. All we need to do is tell her and she'll be fine."

"Let's hope so," I say, looking at the door at the end of the hall. "We're almost there, so it will not be long before we can talk with her about it."

When we reach the door, I knock on it, causing the Head to say, "Come in," before the door slides open. The two of us step inside. I look around at our surroundings as we do so, in order to get a good look at where we are, because I have only been inside this room a few times and am not as familiar with it as I'd like to be.

The Head's room is not terribly different from most of the rooms in this abandoned apartment building: Small, with a leaky ceiling, rotted floor, and peeling wallpaper that reveals the rotted wall underneath. The windows are boarded up and closed, which allows for very little natural light to shine in.

Still, I can see that the Head has been making an effort to clean up the place. The lights, for example, appear to work, even though most of them do not work in the other parts of the building. An old, dusty carpet has been thrown on the floor, hiding most of the rotting, while a moth-eaten sofa has red sheets covering it, although even those sheets appear worn, based on how faded they appear.

The Head herself, a bald woman in silver robes with a back that appears swollen, is sitting on a chair in front of an old, refurbished computer. It was something I had found in one of the rooms of this building, which I was sure wouldn't work when I first found it, but the Head had taken it and fixed it in an hour.

I catch a glimpse of what she is looking at—a map of Xeeon—before she closes it and turns to look at us.

"Lanresia, J997," says the Head, nodding at us both as I close the door behind us. "It is good to see you here. Was the mission a success?"

"Absolutely, ma'am," says Lanresia, nodding. "We kidnapped Xacron-Ah without anyone being the wiser. He's currently tied up in the basement of this very building even as we speak."

"Excellent," says the Head. "This is the best news I have heard in a long time. Already I am thinking of the ways in which we can take advantage of Xacron-Ah and his knowledge."

The Head rubs her hands together in eagerness as she says that. It is the happiest I have seen her in two and a half weeks. No surprise there, considering how uncertain the times are nowadays.

"We have something else to report as well," says Lanresia. "When we were kidnapping Xacron-Ah, we overheard a conversation that he was having with the Founder."

The Head's eagerness and excitement vanishes instantly. She stands up from her chair, but does not approach us. Instead, she puts her hand inside her robe and begins stroking a piece of paper I know she carries within it. I suspect it is the childish drawing I saw once, back in the Foundation's Delanian base. I still do not understand its significance to her, but I do not bring it up at the moment, because it is irrelevant to our current situation.

"He was?" the Head says. "Was the Founder actually there in person?"

"No, he was not," says Lanresia, shaking her head. "It was a hologram. He was telling Xacron-Ah that they are close to completing the Mission, that it won't be long now before they finish it. He even said it would probably be completed within the next few days."

The Head curses under her breath in a language the mobile Database does not recognize. "Of course. While we have been scattered and disorganized, Reunification has been making progress toward achieving their own goals. Did he specify whether he is referring to their Delanian or Xeeonite base?"

"He didn't say," says Lanresia with a shrug. "I imagine it's both, however, because he sounded confident that the Mission will be completed soon, and we know that it cannot be completed without both of their bases."

"This is a grim situation indeed," says the Head. "It means we must work harder and faster than ever to locate and stop them before they can get too far along in their wicked schemes. The lives of billions on both worlds depend on it."

"Agreed," I say. "Although if I may ask, what exactly is Reunification looking for that can reunite Dela and Xeeo?"

The Head and Lanresia exchange brief looks that they seem to believe I do not notice, but I do. I recognize those looks; it is how they look at each other when deciding what information to share with me. It is the primary reason why I still cannot trust them entirely, despite working alongside them as closely as I have recently. They still treat me like an outsider, Rakam's remark toward me earlier notwithstanding.

"I suppose it is safe to let you know now," says the Head. "You have earned our trust over the past two and a half weeks, so I will let you know what Reunification is trying to find. Or at least, what we believe they are looking for, anyway, though all of the evidence points suggests that this is what they are searching for."

"All right," I say. "I am listening."

The Head stops stroking the paper in her robes and says, "They are searching for two large rocks, called the Unification Stones. One is hidden on Xeeo, the other on Dela. In the past, the two of them were once one rock, known as the Unity Rock, or simply the Rock for short. The Unity Rock's separation is the reason why Xeeo and Dela separated. So long as the two Stones remain separated, Xeeo and Dela will continue to be separate worlds."

"So Reunification believes that they can reunite the worlds by bringing the two halves back together?" I say.

"Exactly," says the Head. "Whether that will or will not work, even I do not know. I doubt it will, however, because the two worlds have been separate for so long that I don't think they can be brought back together again without causing the deaths of billions of innocent people."

"I see," I say. "But do you know why the Unity Rock separated in the first place? The mobile Database does not have any files about any 'Unity Rock' or 'Unification Stones.'"

"That's because knowledge of the Stones was lost for thousands of years after the separation occurred," said the Head. "Even us at the Foundation still don't know for certain if they still exist, though it seems likely based on the evidence we've gathered. As for how the Unity Rock originally separated … that is not something you need to know."

"On the contrary, it seems very relevant to our current situation," I say. "How did you even learn of the separation? Did someone tell you about it?"

The Head looks increasingly agitated by my questions, even though they seem rather reasonable to me. She just looks away and says, "Maybe I will tell you later, after we rescue Kojama."

I open my mouth to say that I would rather talk about this now, but then Lanresia speaks up, saying, "Sorry to interrupt your conversation, Head, but I just wanted to let you know that we also learned that Kojama is still alive." She smiles. "That means he survived the massacre at the Xeeonite base, so the massacre wasn't a complete loss to the Foundation, at least."

The Head looks at Lanresia in surprise. "He did? Where is he now? What is his condition?"

"We don't really know the answers to those questions," says Lanresia. "We overheard Xacron-Ah telling the Founder that he has arrested Kojama and is going to have him executed in the morning on trumped up charges."

"Kojama must be held in one of the city's prisons," says the Head. "But did Xacron-Ah say the exact time that this execution would take place?"

"No, he did not," says Lanresia, shaking her head. "He only

said it will be in the morning."

"That is vague and unhelpful," says the Head, rubbing her forehead in frustration. "But regardless, I believe we should make finding and rescuing Kojama our top priority. He is a valuable agent and would prove enormously helpful to us, especially in our current situation."

"But how do we find him?" Lanresia asks. "And even if we do find him, how can we guarantee that we will be able to break him out of prison before the time of his execution?"

"I can connect with the Database and search for any files on Kojama," I offer, tapping the side of my head. "The Database has files on every criminal ever arrested by the J bots. It should not take me long to—"

"No," says the Head, holding up a hand to silence me. "If you connect to the Database, then everyone will know you are here and they will track you down and find us. That will ruin everything. No, I know a different and better way of figuring out where Kojama is."

"And what is that, ma'am?" asks Lanresia.

The Head points at the floor beneath our feet. "Xacron-Ah. We can interrogate him and make him tell us where Kojama is and what time his execution is scheduled for."

"Great idea, ma'am," says Lanresia. "Who should interrogate him?"

The Head strokes her chin again. "I think—"

I hold up a hand. "I can do it."

The Head and Lanresia look at me, apparently surprised by my sudden decision to volunteer.

"Why do you want to interrogate him?" asks the Head.

"Because I have had to interrogate criminals before," I say. "It is a common procedure among J bots, especially when dealing with criminals who do not wish to talk but who have very important information that we need to know. I thus have a variety of interrogation techniques and skills at my disposal that I can use to make Xacron-Ah tell us everything we need to know about Kojama and Reunification itself."

"He has a point," says Lanresia. "I've heard many stories about the J bots and their interrogation techniques. They are supposed to be masters at it. I don't see why we can't let J997 interrogate Xacron-Ah."

The Head, however, does not seem as supportive of the idea as Lanresia is. She looks at me carefully for a moment, as if thinking that I am trying to deceive her, and then folds her arms across her chest and sighs.

"While I would like to do it myself, I really do not have the time to be interrogating our captives," says the Head. "Which is to say, J997, that you have my approval to interrogate Xacron-Ah however you see fit. Just don't kill or critically injure him. I have plans for Xacron-Ah, plans that will not work if he is dead."

I nod and say, "Of course. I will begin immediately, unless you have something else to discuss with me first."

"At the moment, no," says the Head. She hesitates, then says, "But I admit, I do wonder if Xacron-Ah is telling the truth. If Kojama was indeed being executed, I would think that the *Xeeon Daily* would report it. I've been keeping track of the news all day every day ever since we arrived in Xeeon and I have not seen any mention of the execution of a criminal scheduled for the morning."

"He was bragging to the Founder about it, ma'am," says Lanresia. "It doesn't make sense for him to brag about catching Kojama if he actually hasn't. He even claimed to have framed Kojama for that massacre in the Jaws a few weeks ago. Kojama's identity was probably not revealed to the press so any remaining Foundation agents—namely, us—don't learn of it and try to save him in time."

"Wait," says the Head. "I do recall seeing an article in the *Xeeon Daily* that reported that the Jaws massacre killer was arrested and was scheduled to be executed this morning. Are you telling me that the killer and Kojama are one and the same?"

"Of course they're not," says Lanresia. She scowls at the floor, as though Xacron-Ah's face is staring up at her. "I said that Xacron-Ah *framed* Kojama for the massacre."

"I am sorry," says the Head. "I must not have heard you correctly. Nonetheless, this means that we cannot delay interrogating Xacron-Ah for even another second, because I have no doubt that the J bots will do everything in their power to ensure that Kojama's execution goes right on schedule."

"Of course they will," I say. "We are very orderly and scheduled. Everything goes according to schedule no matter what. Even the Mayor's kidnapping will not stall the execution."

"But you must still be careful, J997," says the Head. "Xacron-Ah may not be the most intelligent or cunning of foes, but he is still an agent of Reunification, which means that he no doubt has many clever tricks up his sleeves."

"I doubt he will be that clever," I say. "He injected himself with too much super speed and was barely conscious even after we manipulated him into coming with us. He likely doesn't have enough reason left to resist even the gentlest of interrogation techniques."

"If you say so," says the Head. "Anyway, you should leave now and interrogate him. If Kojama is scheduled to be executed later in the morning, then we don't have much time in which to save him."

I nod and turn to leave. Lanresia also turns to leave, but then the Head says, "Lanresia, I want you to stay here. I have something important to talk with you about in private."

Lanresia stops and looks at me. I shrug, seeing as I do not need her or anyone else with me when I am interrogating Xacron-Ah. I do not even know why she is looking at me for help, although the two of us have grown somewhat close over the last two and a half weeks due to how we have often been paired up on missions together.

"Sure, Head," says Lanresia, turning to face the Head again. "What do you want to talk about?"

"I will tell you once J997 leaves," says the Head. "But before you leave, J997, can you give me Xacron-Ah's com-watch? I would like to study it and see what information he might be keeping on it. It could be even more useful than whatever is inside his head."

That seems like a reasonable request to me, so I pull out the com-watch from my chest compartment and toss it to her over Lanresia's head. The Head catches the com-watch with ease and then turns it over in her hands, like she is trying to make sure it is real.

Then she looks at me over Lanresia's shoulder and nods, a clear sign for me to leave.

RETALIATION

Not that the Head needs to tell me that. I cross the room back to the door, open it, and exit. Even before I fully close the door, however, I hear Lanresia and the Head begin speaking. I am tempted to listen in on their conversation; however, they will easily catch me if I simply stand here and listen.

Instead, I hold up my hand. The palm opens up and a tiny, almost invisible little recorder, shaped like a delane penny, appears in my hand. It is an ant, a type of miniature recording device that I can place somewhere to record any noise or conversation that I wish.

I am aware that this counts as eavesdropping; however, I no longer want to be kept in the dark anymore about the Foundation's other activities, whatever those may be. If they still do not trust me enough to let me in on everything, then I will simply collect the information I want whether they want me to or not; besides, this could potentially help me later on, after this whole mess is over with. Despite my alliance with the Foundation, I am still a J bot at heart and do not wish to be part of an organization that has broken several laws so far (among other things, disabling my connection to the Database, which is a crime punishable by up to thirty years in prison with a 300,000 digit fine for the perpetrator). This ant may provide useful evidence for when I return to the force and need to prove where I have been for two and a half weeks.

I then place the ant on the floor. It crawls under the crack beneath the door, so small that even my optics have a hard time following it. I doubt either the Head or Lanresia will notice; the two sound as though they are already absorbed in their conversation, whatever it may be about. I make a mental note to retrieve it later, perhaps after I interrogate Xacron-Ah.

Then I turn and walk down the hall toward the staircase. As I do so, I reach into my chest compartment, where I usually keep important evidence for crimes, and pull out a small, cracked gray skyras ring, slightly stained with blood. I turn it over in my hands, though I pay little attention to it.

This ring belongs—or belonged, I should say—to a Foundation agent known as Palos. She was the first agent I met, when she saved me from Jornan ah Kona and her vile lizard humanoids. While never close, Palos and I did work together to delay Reunification's mining efforts in the Winterlands on Dela. Unfortunately, Palos was killed by Kalcan, the arctic vampire who is in charge of Reunification's Delanian operations, and the only thing I managed to recover from her death was this gray teleportation skyras ring that she used to wear.

I have zero emotional attachment to her, seeing as I am a robot without feelings. Still, I keep her ring with me, because Palos was an innocent woman unjustly murdered by a vampire. It is evidence that I will use someday when I drag Kalcan before the court of law for his murder. It reminds me to keep going, no matter how grim our situation seems, because to give up now would be to condemn Xeeo and Dela to the terrible fate that Reunification seeks to inflict upon the two worlds.

My mind turns to other subjects as I walk down the stairs. After I was rescued by the Head, we spent a week searching for any surviving members of the Foundation. We did find a few—such as Rakam, who had fled to one of Xeeon's ghettos to avoid being caught—but not nearly as many as we hope. At least, our numbers are so low that there is no way we can possibly hope to take on Reunification in a direct confrontation, especially when you take into consideration Reunification's army of those lizard humanoids from before.

The reason we left Dela to go to Xeeo is so we can kidnap Xacron-Ah, because it is the only way a group as small as ours can hope to strike a blow against Reunification. By holding Xacron-Ah hostage, we are hoping to force Reunification to negotiate with us; or rather, we wish to destroy them. I do not know the full details yet about how we will do that—which is yet another secret that the Foundation is keeping from me—but I guess it will involve blackmailing Reunification in some way, possibly by threatening to expose their existence to the public, although I don't know that for sure.

Anyway, I have reached the bottom of the stairs and am now walking to the basement. It takes me only a few seconds to go down the steps to the basement door, where I find Rakam standing guard. She looks sleepy, likely due to having to stay up all night. I have noticed that most of the Foundation's remaining agents have not slept well since I allied with the group two weeks ago; in fact, I don't think that the Head has slept at all since we arrived in Xeeo.

"Hello, Rakam," I say as I approach her. "I am here to interrogate Xacron-Ah in order to learn the location of Kojama's execution."

"Did the Head give you permission to do that?" asks Rakam.

"Yes," I say. "She did. Will you please open the door so I can go in there and begin the interrogation? We have very little time to waste, so it is imperative that I begin the interrogation as soon as possible."

"All right," says Rakam. She turns to the door and swipes a key card through it, causing a small *click* sound to emit from the lock, which means that the door is unlocked. She then steps aside and says, "Go on in, and don't show him any mercy."

I find Rakam's venomous tone surprising, seeing as she has always appeared to me to be an upbeat and kind individual. Then again, it seems to me that everyone here holds Kojama with utmost respect, so it is perhaps not so surprising that she wants me to show Xacron-Ah no mercy for arresting Kojama on trumped up charges.

I walk up to the door, which slides open with no effort on my part, and step into the room. The door slides closed behind me and I find myself alone in the basement with Xacron-Ah.

I have not been in the basement very many times, so I take a moment to observe my surroundings. It is a small, dingy room, with little lighting save for a single bulb flickering on the ceiling. My thermometer says that the temperature is around 90 degrees; not burning, but hotter than the rest of the building. This is due to the lack of proper ventilation in this room, which allows heat to be caught in it.

The heat does not bother me, however, because as a J bot I can withstand far hotter temperatures than 90 degrees. Xacron-Ah, on the other hand, is sweating in the chair he is tied to. He is clearly overheated, but I am not going to cool him off. I believe he will be easier to interrogate this way.

Walking over to Xacron-Ah, I notice that he is still unconscious. That will not do. I must wake him up if he is going to tell us anything.

So I grab the back of Xacron-Ah's head and force him up to

look at me. Then I slap his face as hard as I can, causing him to start and groan in pain. In fact, I slap him so hard that the imprint of my hand is clear on his cheek.

Blinking rapidly, Xacron-Ah looks at me with dazed, drugged eyes. He barely seems aware of his surroundings or who I am. That does not surprise me. Overdosing super speed can cause an individual to lose all awareness of his surroundings and become incapable of recognizing anyone, even close friends and family members. It seems unlikely to me that he used even one pint of super speed earlier, which means that Xacron-Ah's body is likely not very good at handling the drug.

"Are you awake?" I say. "Xacron-Ah, are you awake?"

Xacron-Ah groans and tries to move, but the ropes keeping him bound to his chair prevent him from moving. "Uh, where am I? What's going on? Who are you?"

I seem to have misjudged how drugged he is, because his awareness appears to be returning rapidly; that is fine by me. It is easier to get factual information out of someone who can think than someone who cannot.

I let go of Xacron-Ah's head and say, "I am J997, a J bot law enforcer. We have never met, but I know all about you due to my position in the force."

Xacron-Ah blinks several times. His eyes are bloodshot, which, in addition to his sweating, makes him look ill. "What the? A J bot? J997? Aren't you the one that Kalcan told me about?"

"The one and the same," I say, gesturing at myself.

Xacron-Ah's eyes widen as understanding dawns in his eyes. "Wait. Kalcan told me you're working with the Foundation. And this room ..." He looks around wildly, like a Grand Lizard trapped in a cage. "This isn't my room. This isn't in Reunification's base, either. This … is this where the Foundation is?"

"I will not answer your questions about the location of this room," I say. "Instead, it will be you who will answer my questions."

Xacron-Ah shakes his head and moans. "Oh, I've got a killer headache. Shouldn't have injected so much super speed into my veins all at once like that. Oh god."

Sensors indicate that Xacron-Ah is telling the truth about his headache (another side effect of the super speed drug), but seeing as I have no way to treat his symptoms at the moment—nor do I have any interest in doing so—I ignore his complaints.

"Your headache is irrelevant, Mayor," I say. "What is relevant, however, is your knowledge of the location of Kojama's execution, which you will tell me about whether you want to or not."

Xacron-Ah looks up at me with hateful eyes. "Why should I tell you anything? You want to rescue him; is that it?"

"Yes," I say. "We overheard you telling the Founder about your success in capturing Kojama. If you would only tell me where the execution will take place and at what time, then we will not need to waste time interrogating you."

Xacron-Ah shakes his head and looks away. "Never. If you heard me telling the Founder about Kojama, then you should also know what the Founder threatened to do to me if I messed up. Bad enough I let you kidnap me, but if I told you about Kojama's execution, the Founder would kill me."

"Yes, we noticed that your leader is not very gentle or

forgiving of mistakes," I say, "but we do not care, to be frank. Kojama's safety is all that matters to us at the moment and the only way to ensure his safety is for you to tell us where he is currently being held."

"I don't need to," says Xacron-Ah. He gestures at one of his tied-up hands behind him. "What's to stop me from sending a message to the J bots so they can locate me and kill you idiots? You don't know if I have some kind of message sending device under my skin."

I grab his wrist and squeeze it so tightly that Xacron-Ah actually yells in pain. I pay little attention to his yells, however, because I focus on his wrist, which, while large and strong, feels like an ordinary human wrist.

"Nice bluffing, Mayor, but I can tell you are an untouched," I say as I take my hand off his wrist. "That makes sense, of course, seeing as you are a native of Dela, and most Delanian natives dislike having any sort of mechanical or technological implants in their bodies at all."

Xacron-Ah scowls at me, but he does not contradict me, likely because he knows he cannot fool me.

Instead, he says, "Well, I still won't talk. Torture me all you like, but I won't utter a single word. I doubt any amount of pain you inflict upon me will hurt as much as what the Founder can do to me."

I tilt my head to the side. "I see."

"Yeah," says Xacron-Ah, whose courage seems to be coming back, as though he thinks he can escape this situation somehow. "Nothing you do to me will make me talk. I've been tough all my life. Even when I was just a common criminal, before I joined

Reunification, I wasn't afraid of the Knights of Se-Dela, even though everyone else was."

"You weren't?" I say. "Why not?"

"'Cause they're a bunch of weaklings in glorified tin cans," says Xacron-Ah. "Yeah, that metalligick armor allows them to do all sorts of weird things, but I was always smarter than them, always clearing out every time they came knocking. And when I became Mayor, I got diplomatic immunity, so those Knights couldn't touch me with a ten foot pole without causing an inter-world incident."

Xacron-Ah speaks with a tough voice and a strong disposition; however, I see through his act right away. This is because I still remember how terrified he appeared earlier after his conversation with the Founder. He may put on a strong and authoritative appearance around others, but in truth, he is a coward who I doubt will require much effort to break.

"So do your worst," says Xacron-Ah, sitting back in his chair with a smug grin on his face. "Besides, I know that you J bots don't commit cold-blooded torture. Goes against your programming. So you can act all tough and threatening as you like, but you can't scare me."

"It is true that we J bots typically avoid torture, mostly due to the public perception of torture as an immoral tool with which to interrogate criminals with," I say, nodding. "But that does not mean that we J bots have not come up with other ways of getting criminals to talk."

I raise my hand, causing Xacron-Ah to laugh. "What, are you going to *slap* me again? Yeah, that hurt the first time, but slapping is hardly what I'd call an effective interrogation technique."

"By itself, you are correct," I say. "But I will not simply be slapping you. Watch."

I charge my hand with electricity, causing it to spark and hiss in the air. As I expect, Xacron-Ah almost jumps off his chair, although due to the ropes binding him to it, he is unable to move from his current position.

"What are you doing?" says Xacron-Ah with a gulp. "What's wrong with your hand?"

"Nothing," I say. "All I am doing is charging electricity through my hand."

"I didn't know you stupid robots could do that," says Xacron-Ah, his eyes never leaving my electrified hand.

"It is not actually an ability most J bots have," I say. "What I am doing is taking the electricity that I normally would shoot from my finger tips and am instead simply charging it along the surface of my hands in order to make my next slap more painful than the last."

My voice is calm, but Xacron-Ah begins sweating and even trembling in his chair anyway. His breathing becomes labored and he suddenly begins rocking back and forth in the chair.

"Anything … anything but that," says Xacron-Ah. He looks like he is about to throw up. "Please don't slap me again. I beg of you. Please don't."

I tilted my head to the side. "You seem unusually afraid. Why is that?"

Xacron-Ah takes a deep breath, but when he opens his mouth, he makes a choking noise before taking another deep breath. I have to admit that I am starting to wonder what kind of health problems Xacron-Ah may suffer from. The mobile Database does not tell me much about his health issues; they are not included in his file, likely to protect his privacy.

Still, Xacron-Ah does manage to say, "When … when I was six-years-old … my father was a wizard. Good one, too. Specialized in electricity magic. He'd have five skyras rings, but rather than each one representing a different kind of magic, each one was yellow for electricity."

I nod. "I have heard of those types of wizards. They are called specialists, are they not?"

"How am I supposed to know?" Xacron-Ah snaps. He closes he mouth, like he is holding back his dinner, but after a moment opens it again. "Anyway, my father … he was abusive. Didn't like me at all. Told me I was a freak. Hated my name. Because my mother was a Xeeonite, you see, and she gave me the name 'Xacron' after her own dad. The 'Ah' part comes from my dad, who wanted me to embrace my Delanian roots."

"Your story is meandering," I say. I bring my electrified hand closer to his face. "Do you want me to help you get to the point?"

"The point," says Xacron-Ah quickly, now speaking so fast that even I have a hard time catching his every word, "is that my father used his rings to abuse me. Little things at first; a jolt here, a jolt there. Then as I got older, he became worse and worse, until some nights he'd almost fry me. God I hated him."

"I am sorry to hear that," I say. "What happened to your father?"

"Old man was killed in a lightning storm," says Xacron-Ah. He chuckles. "Ironic, isn't it? My dad, who loved electricity, was done in by the magic he thought he controlled. Idiot."

Though Xacron-Ah spoke with some satisfaction about his

father's untimely death, he is still quite pale and sickly.

"Anyway," says Xacron-Ah, shaking his head. "Point is, I'm afraid of … afraid of electricity."

I stroke my chin with my other hand. "Interesting. Neither the Database nor its mobile equivalent mention your fear of electricity in their files on you."

"That's because I didn't tell anyone about it," says Xacron-Ah. He shudders. "Do you know how difficult it's been for me to live in Xeeon, where everyone uses electricity for everything? Only reason I even took on the job of Mayor is because the Founder ordered me to. Otherwise, I'd be back home in Dela, where there isn't as much electricity. Probably somewhere rural; I've heard that some of the larger cities are using more electricity."

"Interesting," I say. "If I promise not to slap you with my electrified hand, will you agree to tell me the location of Kojama's execution?"

Xacron-Ah bites his lower lip. He appears to be giving my offer serious consideration, which is good, because this means that I will not need to spend so much time interrogating him. Most interrogations tend to last much longer than this; however, if he does accept my offer, that will not bother me in the slightest.

But then, to my disappointment, Xacron-Ah shakes his head again and says, "No. Never. Electricity scares me, but you know what scares me more? The Founder's wrath. He's as crazy as a super speed abuser. You don't know what he's done to people who have failed him in the past. Absolutely brutal. Makes the Destroyer look like a saint."

I should slap Xacron-Ah now. Pain is an excellent motivator for getting someone to tell you what you need to know, even if the victim in question puts on a brave face at first and pretends otherwise. I have met many criminals in the past who act like nothing can break them, but when faced with the tiniest of pain, immediately fall apart and tell you everything you need to know (and more, in the cases of particularly weak or cowardly criminals).

But I want to know more about the Founder. I know that he is the true leader of Reunification, who controls the entire organization behind the shadows and has since the organization's genesis many years ago. Yet I know little else about him, which is not good, because he is too important an individual to have incomplete records on.

Yes, I know I am supposed to get information on Kojama's location—and I will—but to me personally, learning more about the Founder is more important than helping Kojama. Despite my alliance with the Foundation, their goals and mine still do not exactly align; therefore, I will see if I can get Xacron-Ah to tell me what he knows about the Founder.

So I pull back my electrified hand, saying, "Why don't you tell me more about the Founder, Mayor? The Foundation hasn't told me much about him, although I do not know if that is because they are as ignorant of him as I am or if they are simply keeping their facts about him a secret from me."

"Never," says Xacron-Ah. "I will never—"

Without warning, my hand flies through the air toward his face. He screams in fear, but at the last possible second, I stop my hand exactly one inch from his face. He is sweating more profusely now than ever; in fact, his suit is starting to get stained by his sweat, especially around the armpits. He even makes hurtling sounds, but nothing comes out of his mouth.

"Okay, okay, I'll tell you everything I know about the Founder," says Xacron-Ah. He takes a deep shuddering breath, his eyes locked on my hand. "Just ... just take that damn hand away from me, okay? I can't even think straight with that thing hovering an inch from my face."

I nod and pull my hand away. I lower my hand to my side, but do not shut off the electricity. My power is currently at 89%, after all, and my electrified hand barely uses any of that. It is a useful weapon to have with me, especially in this situation.

"Start with the Founder's real name," I say. "What is it?"

Xacron-Ah gulps. "I ... I don't know. No one does. Not even Kiriah knows. He insists we all call him the Founder. He might not even have a real name for all we know. He acts like the Founder is his actual name."

Useless information. Nonetheless, I continue to press him for information, because there is a still a real possibility that Xacron-Ah might know something important. "Where did he come from: Dela or Xeeo? Which planet is he a native of?"

"N-Neither," says Xacron-Ah with a shudder. "The Founder said he came from the world that existed before Dela or Xeeo."

"That is impossible," I say. "That would make the Founder thousands, maybe even tens of thousands, of years old, depending on how long ago Dela and Xeeo were split."

"He's immortal," says Xacron-Ah. "That's another thing I know about him. He can't die. You can stab him, shoot him, slice him up, toss him into a pit of lava ... but he comes back. He *always* comes back. And he *always* gets his revenge on those who try to kill him."

"Interesting," I say, stroking my chin once more. "How does he accomplish that? Is he a skyras wizard?"

"Nope," says Xacron-Ah, shaking his head. "He can use skyras, but he doesn't need even one skyras ring to do it. He just waves his hands and makes stuff happen. Doesn't even have to say anything to cast a spell, either."

"That is equally nonsensical," I say. "Delanian magic can only be used via skyras rings. Skyras energy itself can of course be gathered and used to power machines and the like, but you need a ring to perform magic with it—yet you claim that the Founder can use magic without one?"

"I don't know how, but he can," Xacron-Ah insists. He looks around, like he thinks someone might be eavesdropping on us, and then leans forward and whispers, "He's a freak. I'll tell you that much."

"A freak?" I repeat. "Well, he certainly does sound unusual, to be sure. Tell me: how did he end up with a half-mechanical face? Do you know what accident caused that to happen to him and how long ago it may have happened?"

"Hell if I know," says Xacron-Ah with a shrug. "The Founder's not much of a talker, but if you ask me, he's way more mechanical than human. Doesn't seem to feel emotion half the time, except when we fail, and then he's furious and punishes us as a lesson to the rest."

"What is his connection to the Head of the Foundation?" I ask. "Do you know it?"

Xacron-Ah again shrugs, but that shrug does not appear genuine to me. "Nope. Didn't even know the two knew each other until you just mentioned it to me."

Sensors indicate that his heart rate is increasing, which means that he is lying. He likely knows far more than he lets on, which means that I should go in for the kill.

"Do not lie to me," I say. I hold up my electrified hand again. "Unless you want me to slap you for real this time. I find that that works in getting people to tell me the truth."

"No, wait!" Xacron-Ah says, trembling in his chair so much that he almost falls backward as he leans away from my electrified hand. "I'll tell you what I know, I'll tell you what I know. Or, at least, what I've *heard*, anyway."

Lowering my electrified hand, I say, "Continue."

"All right," says Xacron-Ah. He takes a deep breath and then says, "I don't know if you know, but Kiriah and I meet about once every three months at a cafe in Xeeon called Crossways Cafe. We do this as a way to stay in touch and also trade information and updates on our individual missions' progress."

I can tell, with the way Xacron-Ah's heart rate beats and the tone in his voice, that he obviously considers these in-person meetings to be a bit more than merely business. But I say nothing, because Xacron-Ah appears to be about to tell me everything I need to know.

"On one of these meetings last year, Kiriah told me something strange," says Xacron-Ah. "She said to me, 'Xac, can you keep a secret?' and I said, 'Of course I can. What is it?' and she leaned forward, looking very serious, and said, 'Promise you won't mention this to anyone, least of all the Founder.' And of course I would never betray her confidence, so I nod and reassure her that I can keep whatever secret she tells me."

Even I can see the irony in our current situation, seeing as he is betraying Kiriah's confidence by relating this story to me. Although, in truth, it does not bother me, because his going against his word is what will give me the information I need to understand and stop the Founder better.

"So Kiriah says, 'Last night, I went to the Founder's chambers in order to deliver an in-person report to him, since he tends to like those better than paper or electronic reports, especially from me, but when I went down there, I heard something.'

"'Heard what?' I asked.

"'I heard the Founder sitting alone in his chamber ... crying.' And she said that with a very serious look on her face, which made me know she wasn't making this up.

"'Crying?' I said. 'How can the Founder cry? I didn't even know he could cry.'

"'He was,' Kiriah said. 'And he kept repeating this one name over and over: Kara. He went on and on about how he missed her, how he wanted to end his tortured existence if it will bring him back together with her again, how he wants nothing more than their relationship to be mended again. It was scary; for a moment there, I thought he really was going to kill himself.'

"'I was so worried that I knocked on the door and asked him to come out. When he did, he looked like he hadn't been crying at all, although I noticed tear stains running down the organic side of his face.'"

"Is that all Kiriah told you?" I say.

Xacron-Ah nods. "Yep. The only thing else she told me is that the Founder forbid her to tell anyone else about his crying, but she went ahead and told me without letting the Founder know, which is why she wanted to keep it a secret; that really surprised me, because I always thought Kiriah was the most loyal of us all to the Founder. So seeing her go against his orders, even on a fairly trivial issue like this, was something else."

Xacron-Ah sounds impressed when he says that, as if he admires Kiriah's bravery. Considering how he blasted the Founder earlier, I understand why.

"Who is Kara?" I say.

"No idea," says Xacron-Ah with a shrug. "Kiriah said she thinks it might be the Head's real name, but since neither of us know the Head or have even met that old witch, I don't know. 'Course, it could be someone else completely, but maybe not. It's just a random theory Kiriah came up with; might not have any truth to it at all."

Interesting. Very interesting. If Xacron-Ah is telling the truth, then it appears to me that the relationship between the Founder and the Head is deeper and more complicated than I realize. Were they friends? Or perhaps lovers in the past? Or did they have a different relationship entirely?

It is impossible to say at this point. I need more facts before I can make any solid conclusions about their relationship. I cannot speak with the Founder, but perhaps I can find a way to learn more from the Head. She is quite reticent, however, especially around me. Maybe the ant I planted earlier will pick up some information on her past, even though I doubt that that is what she is speaking with Lanresia about.

So I say to Xacron-Ah, "Is that all Kiriah told you?"

Xacron-Ah nods hurriedly. "Yes. Please don't slap me."

"I won't," I say. "I can tell you are not withholding any important information from me. You have told me all you know

69

about the Founder, so inflicting pain on you would not make sense at this point."

Xacron-Ah sighs heavily. "Oh, that's a relief."

"But I still need to know about Kojama," I say. "You know, the original reason I came down here to interrogate you."

Xacron-Ah shakes his head. "No. You might have gotten me to talk about the Founder, but you can't make me tell you where that idiot is. And don't bother watching the telescreen news; this is going to be a private execution and I've made sure that the press doesn't know where he is going to be executed."

"I thought you hated the Founder," I say. "I heard you ranting about him earlier, after you finished your meeting with him. You used quite a few curse words to describe him."

"That's because he's an idiot," says Xacron-Ah. He shudders and then looks around again before continuing. "Likes to pretend that he's all wise and understanding, but he's the freakiest and cruelest being I've ever known in my life. And I used to hang out with super speed smugglers; that is, *violent* super speed smugglers who didn't think twice about brutally killing anyone who tried to move in on their turf or take their drugs. He's way worse than all of them combined."

"Then why do you work for him?" I say. "Why not work with us? By giving us all you know about Reunification, you can help us put an end to the Founder's schemes."

"Hell no," says Xacron-Ah. "I work with him because he promised me power. He said that if I helped, I would not only get political power in this world, but also become king of my own empire in the next. He made it sound so good that I didn't think twice about accepting his offer to join and doing whatever he told me to do."

"But you are having second thoughts now?" I say.

"Not exactly," says Xacron-Ah. "It's just that I've started to learn just how cruel and merciless he can really be. Once, when I was visiting our base in the Dead Lands, I saw him beat to death one of our minor agents who failed a pretty minor mission. Then he threw the poor sap into the pit where we keep all of the Lizard-men and didn't let anyone retrieve his remains for two weeks. Not that there was much left to retrieve after two weeks with all of those monsters."

"So you only follow him out of fear," I say.

Xacron-Ah purses his lips. He clearly does not want to say that aloud, but he does not fool me. Fear is a motivating factor for many criminals, especially ones like Xacron-Ah, who are not very intelligent or clever. This means that the Founder is even more dangerous than I originally thought.

"So I won't tell you anything about Kojama's execution," says Xacron-Ah. "I don't like the Founder much, but I hate you Foundation members even more. Kojama in particular has been a thorn in my side for a while now. Glad I finally get to remove it."

"Then it is quite clear to me," I say, raising my electrified hand again, "that if you are not going to willingly tell me about Kojama's murder, I will have to *make* you tell me."

Xacron-Ah again trembles in his chair, but to his credit, he does not break down and beg for mercy like earlier. His eyes merely watch my electrified hand with the same kind of caution with which a human watches a crawling spider. It is almost like his fear of electricity has simply vanished.

But before I can slap him, Xacron-Ah snaps the ropes tying

him to his chair with a shrug of his massive shoulders and lunges toward me even faster than my optics can follow. He slams into me with his shoulder, the blow sending me staggering backwards, but I manage to regain my balance even as Xacron-Ah runs at me again, yelling obscenities at me as he does so.

I try to shoot him with my finger lightning bolts, but Xacron-Ah is upon me again before I can fire. He grabs me by the neck and slams me into the wall. The blow does not actually damage me, due to my powerful metal skin, but it does jar my senses briefly.

Then Xacron-Ah tosses me to the floor and stomps on my chest. That impact also jars my senses, but I grab his foot as soon as its hits me and pull. With a yell, Xacron-Ah falls to the floor and in a second I jump back to my feet.

But Xacron-Ah is much faster than he appears, because he, too, recovers, standing up and dusting off his sweaty jacket. He growls at me like a Grand Lizard and then charges at me too fast for me to shoot him.

But I do not need to shoot him. Instead, I rear back and punch him in the face as hard as I can with my electrified fist. The blow sends him staggering backwards until he trips over his own large feet and lands flat on his back on the floor.

I do not give him a moment to rest, however. I dash over and pin his arms to the floor with my feet, applying enough pressure to make him cry out in pain and stop resisting. Looking down, I see that my punch did a number on his face; his left eye is swollen and he has some bruises on his face.

He still conscious, however, and is now looking up at me with anger. He can't move, however, because I am applying my full weight to his arms to keep him from going anywhere.

"Get off me, you stupid machine," says Xacron-Ah. "Get off me!"

At that moment, the door to the basement opens and Rakam pokes her head inside and says, "J997, what's going on? I thought I heard figh—"

She stops when she sees me pinning Xacron-Ah to the floor and then gapes.

"The prisoner escaped from his bindings somehow," I say, gesturing at Xacron-Ah below me. "I had to subdue him before he could escape."

Rakam is still gaping at me. So I decide that now is as good an opportunity for a joke as ever, so I run a quick search of *Secrets of Humor* for a good joke for this situation and soon find one.

So I say, "He really had it coming. Like the Rain Man."

Instead of laughter, however, I receive more of those same awkward and confused stares my jokes always seem to get. Even Xacron-Ah stares at me like he is uncertain if he is hearing me correctly.

"Was that … a joke?" says Rakam.

I nod. "Yes. Did I say it wrong?"

Rakam shakes her head, although I can tell she does not find it funny. "No, no, it's just … well, maybe I should just go back to guarding the door, since you clearly seem to have Xacron-Ah under control here yourself."

She slams the door shut before I can say anything. Her behavior puzzles me, but I decide that, as a Jikorian, she must have a different sense of humor than humans. Then again, Xacron-Ah is also human and he is not laughing, although

73

considering how I just beat him down, perhaps that is the reason for his lack of laughter.

"Now," I say, bending over, but still applying pressure on his arms to ensure he will not try to escape from me again. "Tell me the time and location of Kojama's execution."

Xacron-Ah looks like he is going to keep his mouth shut—which means I will need to use advanced interrogation techniques to make him talk—but then he finally says, "Xeeon City Prison. Ten-thirty in the morning. It's going to be a firing squad."

My sensors do not indicate that Xacron-Ah is lying, so it appears that he is telling the truth. Therefore, I must get this information to the Head as soon as possible so she can make a plan of action for how we will rescue Kojama.

But first, I must ensure that Xacron-Ah cannot escape; once I finish that, however, I will go and speak with the Head immediately. And also, of course, listen to my ant and find out just what she and Lanresia are talking about.

Chapter 3

Standing in the Head's room, with my hands at my sides, I watch as the Head considers all of the information I give her. It is not much, seeing as Xacron-Ah only spoke tersely, but it is enough, in my opinion, to form a rescue plan.

Lanresia also stands in the room with us, but she keeps looking over her shoulder at the door. She does not want to leave this room; she is simply worried about Konoa, who we still have not heard from ever since the kidnapping. She is starting to worry that the J bots may have arrested him, but I doubt it myself, seeing as the arrest of a criminal who threw a blind bomb into a crowded street is surely something that would be on the news. Considering how we have not heard anything on the news about Konoa's arrest, I assume he is still free, although where Konoa is at this very moment, I do not know.

The Head is sitting in her chair, her arms folded across her chest. She is staring at the floor, apparently thinking about what I told her. It is hard for me to tell what she is thinking, even harder for me to tell what she is feeling, because my sensors do not seem to work on her in the same way they work on other organics. There is certainly something strange about her, that much I know.

During the silence, I wonder if the Head's name really is Kara. Running that name through the mobile Database, I discover that there are one thousand female humans in Xeeon with that name or a variation thereof (such as Cara, for example). It turns up no results at all on Delanian names, but the mobile Database does state that *Kara* is derived from an Ancient Xeeonish word meaning 'one who separates.' Whether that applies to the Head or not, I am not sure, but it is an interesting fact nonetheless.

As for my ant, it currently lies in little pieces in the cracks of the floor. I discovered that when I first entered the room and attempted to summon it back to my body, only for it to ignore my commands. I then performed a quick, automatic scan of the room while I explained to the Head and Lanresia what I learned from Xacron-Ah without either of them being aware. That is when I discovered the ant in pieces in the cracks in the floor.

I, of course, have not mentioned a word of this to the Head or Lanresia. I do not want either of them knowing just how little I trust the Foundation. Yet I suspect they must know that I put it there; after all, how else could my ant have been destroyed if they had not known of it?

Of course, it is possible that the ant was actually destroyed unknowingly by one of the two; it is, after all, a small thing and very quiet. It would not be the first time that a J bot ant was accidentally destroyed by someone who did not know it was there. That may be why neither of them have said a word about it to me yet.

Finally, the Head looks up at us and says, "Xacron-Ah said that the execution is scheduled for ten-thirty in the morning?"

"Yes," I say. "And do not bet on my fellow J bots delaying the execution due to Xacron-Ah's disappearance. Criminal punishments are never delayed for any reason among us J bots, and that includes executions, both public and private."

"Then that means there isn't much time left," says the Head. "J997, you know about Xeeon City Prison, don't you?"

"I do," I say. "In my time, I have delivered many convicted criminals to that place. It's the largest and most well-guarded prison in the entire city; in fact, it regularly tops the list of the ten best prisons in all of Xeeo and usually makes it into the top five prisons in the two worlds. It will not be easy to break into, even with my knowledge of its layout and security systems."

"No, it won't," says the Head, nodding. "But we must do it anyway. Kojama is an important asset to the Foundation. With his help, we would stand a far better chance against Reunification than we currently do."

Lanresia looks at me anxiously. "J997, do you know if it is possible for us to break in and save Kojama before the execution?"

"It is possible," I say. "But it would be extremely difficult. Four hundred and fifty J bots patrol both the interior and exterior of the prison every day; it has the most advanced security systems in the city; and it is located right in the middle of Xeeon, in a crowded area, which will make it hard to sneak Kojama out or any of our own agents in."

"Not to mention how it is home to hundreds of actual criminals," the Head adds. "Vicious ones, too, like Roda the Slicer, who murdered a dozen people before being caught and sentenced to life in prison last year."

"The criminals will not be much of an issue," I say. "They are locked away and unable to harm even themselves. It is the guards we need to worry about. Unlike most J bots, they shoot to kill; if they see a prisoner attempting to escape or someone aiding in a prisoner's escape, they have full authority to kill them on the spot, no questions asked."

Lanresia looks sickened by that idea. She says, "Really? That seems cruel."

"Only the worst of the worst are put in that prison," I say. "Therefore, if we are unable to capture them, it is sometimes better to kill them so that they cannot break the law or terrorize the innocent anymore. Regrettably, it is sometimes the only way to deal with criminals as violent as they."

"It doesn't matter," says the Head. She unfolds her hands and rests them on her knees. "What matters is that they will shoot us if they catch us in the middle of rescuing Kojama. We have to figure out a way to get someone on the inside and have them save Kojama before his execution."

Lanresia looks at me. "Why don't you do it, J997? You are a J bot. You know and understand the prison's layout and security systems better than anyone here."

"True, but I am not supposed to be seen in the general public," I say. "Remember, at this point, I am a wanted criminal in Dela and have few fans here in Xeeo. It is very likely that I would be captured quite easily if I tried to break into the prison, after which they would hook me up to the Database and discover everything about us. And by the time I manage to convince them to stop Reunification, it will probably be far too late, because the Founder made it sound like they were very close to completing their Mission."

"J997 makes a good point," says the Head. "Sending him in right now would only hurt, not help, us. But we do need to send *someone* in. The question is, who? Who among us would be able to infiltrate that place without arousing any unnecessary suspicion?"

At that moment, the door to the room burst open and Rakam staggers through it. She is panting, like she has run a mile, and she is also sweating the green sweat that all Jikorians secrete when they are hot.

"What's the problem?" says the Head, standing up as we all turn to look at Rakam. "What happened?"

"Konoa ..." Rakam takes a deep breath. "He's back. He just came in a few seconds ago."

Lanresia's face breaks out into a large smile. "Great. Where is he?"

"Downstairs getting something to eat," says Rakam. "He says no one followed him, so we should be all right."

"That's good to hear," says the Head. "Does he have anything else to report?"

"No," says Rakam, shaking her head. "Nothing else. He's just tired and hungry from the events of the night."

The Head strokes her chin, clearly deep in thought. While I do not know the Head very well, I can read her expression clearly enough to know that this recent bit of news has gotten her thinking.

Then she lowers her hand from her chin and says, "Rakam, go back downstairs and tell Konoa to come up here. I have a new mission for him that I think he will be perfect for."

A few minutes later, the Head finishes explaining to Konoa what we have learned from Xacron-Ah. Konoa—a tall, thin man

79

with a scarred face, who is currently holding his skull mask in his right hand—listens intently to every word. Even so, I can tell he doesn't see where the Head is going with all of this, although I can.

When the Head finishes, Konoa scratches the back of his head and says, "Well, what are we waiting for, then? Why don't we go and break Kojama out of prison before they execute him? It doesn't sound like we have much time left before they kill him."

"We will," says the Head. "We will. But first, we need someone to do it."

Konoa points at me. "J997 can—"

"We've already discussed this," says Lanresia. She is holding Konoa's left hand, which she grabbed almost as soon as Konoa entered the room earlier, and does not appear to be likely to let go of it anytime soon. "J997 would be a liability due to the public perception of him, as well as the information he knows about the Foundation. He is too suspicious to directly interact with his fellow J bots at the moment."

"Oh, right," says Konoa. "Well, who is supposed to save Kojama, then?"

Unsurprisingly, the Head points at Konoa. "You."

Konoa and Lanresia look at the Head in surprise, but I do not. It was obvious to me that the Head was filling Konoa in on what Lanresia and I learned in order to get him ready for his mission, but I say nothing, as I want to hear the Head's reasoning for this decision.

Sitting down in her wobbly wooden chair, the Head says, "The reason I have chosen you to break into the Prison is because you are already a wanted criminal due to your actions tonight.

You are all over the news, in fact."

The Head turns to her computer, inputs a few commands in the holographic keyboard projecting from underneath the monitor, and a clip from the *Xeeon Daily* news program immediately starts playing. It shows a clip of Konoa, still wearing that mask, running into a dark alley between two buildings as several J bots fly after him in pursuit.

A female voice—likely the news anchor reporting the event—is speaking over the clip. "As you can see, this footage captured by officer J876 shows the mysterious masked bomber fleeing into this alleyway, with six officers in pursuit. It is still unknown who this man is, but officials have asked anyone who recognizes him to please come forward and report what you know to your local police station."

The Head taps another key on the holographic board and the clip pauses. She then looks back at Konoa. "See? Because you are a wanted criminal, the last place that anyone expects you to go is the most impregnable prison in the entire city. That is what makes you the perfect choice for the job."

Konoa bites his lower lip and looks at Lanresia, who smiles and nods at him.

Then he looks at the Head and says, "While I am of course not against rescuing Kojama, I'm not certain you have thought this through completely, ma'am. For example, I know nothing about the Xeeon City Prison, so how am I supposed to break Kojama out of it?"

"Easy," says the Head. She points at me. "J997 will accompany you and give you the instructions you need to escape and get past all of the guards and security measures you and

Kojama may face on the inside."

Konoa looks at me in surprise, then looks back at the Head. "Well, that's not a bad idea, but—"

"Head, we have already established that my presence in the prison would be more of a liability than a help," I say. "Yes, I can tell Konoa about all of the inner-workings of the prison, but that is different from actually being there in person with him to guide him through whatever obstacles or challenges he may face while in there."

"That's why we are going to get you in there without anyone, even your fellow J bots, ever knowing even if they catch Konoa," says the Head. She then opens the top drawer of the desk that her computer is set open and digs through it for a moment before pulling out some kind of small metallic object. "Look at this."

The object in the Head's hand is tiny; so tiny, in fact, that it is almost invisible against her pale skin. It resembles a computer chip, but it does not resemble any computer chip I have seen before.

Konoa and Lanresia must not know what it is, either, because Konoa simply stares at it without comprehension, while Lanresia says, "What is it? A computer chip?"

"It's far than a simple computer chip," says the Head. "It is a personal invention of mine. I call it the Third Eye, so named because it is placed on your forehead and allows someone else to view your surroundings with you."

"So it's essentially a micro camera?" says Konoa. "That doesn't seem terribly helpful to me."

"It's more than a micro camera," the Head insists. "You can download an AI onto it and the AI will not only be able to view its surroundings, but also interact with the Third Eye's user via a connection to the brain, which sends messages to the user similar to telepathy. It is like having a second soul in your body."

"That is an amazing piece of tech you've got there, Head," says Konoa. He tears his gaze from it and looks directly at the Head. "But I still don't understand how it is supposed to help us."

"Then let me explain in the plainest words I know," says the Head. She gestures at me. "J997 will download his AI into the chip. We will then surgically attach the chip to your brain, Konoa. Once we do that, J997, in the Third Eye, will be able to help you break into and navigate the Prison in order to rescue Kojama."

I hold up my hand, because several questions occur to me as I listen to her explanation. "Hold it. How do we know this Third Eye of yours will work? Has it been sufficiently tested for any possible glitches or bugs that might interfere with its effectiveness?"

"Of course I have been testing it," says the Head. "This particular creation of mine has been in development for five years now. It is hard—not impossible, but hard—to create a device capable of holding the vast AI of a J bot while simultaneously being small enough to hide in the body of a human being without detection. We would have done more research and development on it, but unfortunately we were forced to abandon all of that when Reunification attacked and destroyed the Xeeonite base."

"How long have you had it?" I ask. "Why have you never mentioned this to us before? And where did you get it?"

"Lanresia gave it to me," says the Head, nodding at her. "When she first arrived in the Delanian base to report the attack on our Xeeonite branch, she gave me this chip because she said that one of our engineers—who unfortunately ended up dying during the assault—gave it to her with instructions to deliver it to me."

"That's true," says Lanresia, nodding both of her heads. "I *did* give the Head that chip, but I didn't know what it was at the time or why it was so important. I'm quite glad I listened to that engineer now, though."

"Lucky us," says Konoa. He rubs his forehead. "Well, I can't say I am looking forward to having J997 in my head, telling me what to do, but if it will help us save Kojama, I am all for it."

"I, too, think it is a good idea," I say. "My only concern, however, is that my fellow J bots will discover it and destroy it if they arrest Konoa. We J bots have special tools we can use to scan the body of an organic being for any technological add-ons or implants. Assuming we break into the Prison, I will probably be found out right away, and removed and possibly even destroyed if I am deemed a large enough threat."

"Good point," says Konoa. "And not to mention that even if we *do* get on the inside, there are still too many J bots for us to get past. That prison is crawling with law enforcers who won't hesitate to shoot prisoners attempting to make an escape."

"The first issue should not be a problem, because you two are supposed to break in and out without being caught, so it doesn't matter if the guards can sense the Third Eye or not," says the Head. "As for the guards, you are correct that they pose a special problem, but that is why we have Xacron-Ah."

"What will Xacron-Ah do for us?" says Konoa. "Are you going to force him to order the J bots to free Kojama for us?"

"No," says the Head. She closes her hand around the chip and pulls it back to her chest. "Xacron-Ah would never do that, even if we threatened him with cold-blooded torture. He's a fool and a coward, but he would never order the J bots to abandon their duties, especially to free a known Foundation agent. And if we tried to contact the J bots, they would track down our signal and overrun our hideout in an attempt to rescue Xacron-Ah."

"Then what is Xacron-Ah supposed to *do*?" says Konoa, in an increasingly agitated voice. "Rot away in the basement of our headquarters?"

"No," says the Head. "Instead, we'll use Xacron-Ah's com-watch to contact Reunification. We will inform them that Xacron-Ah is our hostage and pretend to make demands of them, but in truth, J997 will use the link between us and Reunification to locate Reunification's headquarters, the location of which we will then anonymously report to the J bots."

"I see," I say. "So you are saying that my fellow officers will follow the anonymous tip to Reunification's headquarters in the Dead Lands, correct? And arrest its members, or at least disrupt their activities out there?"

"Correct," says the Head. "The J bots will likely send dozens, maybe even hundreds, of J bots out that way to apprehend Reunification's members. As a result, there will be far fewer J bots—including the Xeeon City Prison guards—here in Xeeon, which will make it easier for us to break into the Prison. Of those that stay behind, very few will expect a wanted criminal like Konoa to try to break in to rescue another criminal."

"Brilliant," says Konoa. "I have to admit, Head, that you seem to have thought of all possible obstacles that could disrupt the plan. I can't see how anything could go wrong with a plan like this."

"Every plan has its flaws, Konoa," says the Head, although she does sound proud of herself anyway. "But thank you nonetheless. I only thought of this within the last half hour or so, when J997 told me about Kojama's location."

I find that unlikely. No organic being can possibly come up with a plan that detailed and so well thought-out in such a short amount of time. I know that the Head is an intelligent woman— she must be, otherwise the Foundation could not have kept itself a secret for so many years—but I find it hard to believe that she made up this plan so quickly. Yet there is no way for her to have spent any significant time thinking through this plan, because she did not know about Kojama's location until now, while Konoa had only just returned from escaping my fellow officers. I am forced to believe her, then, when she claims to have thought up the plan in such a small amount of time, although it makes her more dangerous in my eyes, seeing as anyone who can think that quickly can probably think of even more dangerous plans than that if they want to.

"So what's our first step?" says Konoa.

"Our first step is to contact Reunification and lay out the details of our fake demands to them," says the Head. "After we set the J bots on them, we will download J997's AI into the Third Eye and place it in your brain. And finally, you will break into the prison, where you and J997 will work together to free Kojama."

The way the Head lays it all out, she makes it sound as simple and easy as an oil change. But of course, I doubt any of that will be as easy as she makes it out to be; still, even I must admit that it is a good plan, even the best plan, in our current situation, so I say nothing about its difficulty level, because that will only discourage us.

The Head stands up from her chair and says, "Now, let's get to work. And quickly; we have wasted enough time talking as is. Kojama's execution is soon, so let's put the plan into motion right away."

Chapter 4

When we go down to the basement, we find Xacron-Ah where I left him, still tied up in his chair, his head hanging on his chest. He raises his head when we enter, however, and his one good eye, the one that is not swollen, widens when he sees the Head with us.

"Back again?" says Xacron-Ah when he sees me, though he does not sound as confident as his words suggest. "Going to skip the interrogation and just move onto cold-blooded torture now? Or did you bring your friends to do that for you so you wouldn't have to dirty your little metal fingers?"

The Head shakes her head as I close the door behind us. "No. You have told us everything we want to know. Instead, you are going to help us destroy your friends. But first—"

The Head pulls a soft rubber ball from her robes' pockets and thrusts it into Xacron-Ah's mouth. Xacron-Ah tries to speak, but his voice is muffled by the rubber ball, making it impossible to tell what he is trying to say. I can guess, however, that it is not kind, whatever it is.

"Lanresia," says the Head, holding out her hand to the female elf. "Give me Xacron-Ah's com-watch."

Lanresia, who had taken the com-watch from Rakam earlier, gives the device to the Head. The Head then walks away, to the other side of the room, looking down at the com-watch. She is scrolling through the contact numbers on it, though I wonder if Xacron-Ah is actually dumb enough to keep the contact number for Reunification stored on his com-watch. That seems like a security hazard to me; then again, Xacron-Ah has already shown himself not to be the cleverest Mayor of Xeeon, so maybe he does have Reunification's contact number stored there.

A couple of minutes later, the Head says, "Found it."

Xacron-Ah is watching her with a confused look on his face. He seems unable to comprehend what we are trying to do, which confirms my earlier judgment that he is not a very clever Mayor.

"All right," says the Head. She looks over her shoulder at me. "J997, I want you to be connected to the com-watch as well. I want you to track the location of Reunification's Xeeonite headquarters as I speak with whoever is on the other side. But don't say that or give any indication that that is what you are doing while I speak with whoever we manage to connect with; if they even suspect we're tracking their location, they will cut off our connection with them before we can learn where they are."

"All right," I say. "I can do that. We J bots can sync with com-watches, after all. But I will do it in stealth mode; that way, Reunification's computers will not notice me when I try to locate their location."

The Head nods. "All right. Are you ready to start?"

I hold up a hand and send out a message to the com-watch, asking to sync with it. It takes the com-watch only a second to accept my request, though at the moment there is nothing for me to track because the Head has not contacted Reunification's headquarters yet.

"I am synced with the com-watch now," I say. "I am ready when you are, Head."

Xacron-Ah finally seems to understand what is going on, because he is now cursing at us through his rubber gag; not that I care, because there is nothing he can do to harm us in this situation anyway. Lanresia, however, points a gun at him, causing him to stop cursing immediately.

"All right," says the Head. "Here we go …"

She presses a number on the com-watch's touch screen. A hologram shoots out of the com-watch onto the floor in front of the Head, though it initially only shows the word 'CONNECTING' in large, transparent red letters. Xacron-Ah is sweating again as we all wait for the com-watch to connect.

Then the word 'CONNECTING' changes to 'CONNECTED' and the hologram turns into a screen. On the holographic screen, we see what looks like a central control room, with many computer monitors, some floating and some not. Sitting at one of the still monitors is a dwarf with red hair, but he is not looking at the monitor that he is sitting in front of. He is instead looking directly at us with wild eyes, like a wild animal backed into a corner.

"Who …" the dwarf stumbles over his words. "Who are you and how did you contact us?"

"I am from the Foundation," says the Head. "And I demand an audience with the Founder."

"The Foundation?" says the dwarf in shock. "But the Foundation is—"

"Still alive and well, thank you very much," says the Head. "Anyway, as I said, I demand an audience with the Founder. Go

90

and find him right away. I don't have time to waste talking with simple peons like you."

"Why should I?" says the dwarf. His hand floats over the keyboard in front of him. "Maybe I should just cut off this connection. You aren't the boss of me, after all. I don't need to listen to Foundation trash like *you*."

I hope that the dwarf does not sever the connection, because I am still trying to discover the exact location of their hideout. It is much more difficult than it first appears, as Reunification appears to use a complicated encryption system to keep hackers like myself from tracking down their location. Still, given enough time, I think I can crack it, as their systems are still unaware of my presence and my efforts to hack them.

"Are you certain that you want to do that?" says the Head. "Because we have something of yours that we might be willing to give back if you would deal with us."

"What could you possibly have that we would want?" says the dwarf. "Nothing, that's what. You Foundation agents don't even have a base to call your own anymore."

"You're correct about that," says the Head. "But we do have Xacron-Ah, who we are willing to give back to you in exchange for something we want."

The dwarf's face pales and he glances down at the monitor in front of him. "Oh, uh, well, I see that your connection *is* coming from Xacron-Ah's com-watch, but—"

"But nothing," says the Head forcefully. "We kidnapped Xacron-Ah and he is now our prisoner. Unless you give me the audience with the Founder that I demand, we will never let him go. Got it?"

The dwarf jumps to his feet and says, "Yes, yes, I understand. I will go and inform our leadership about your demands. Please wait."

"All right," says the Head. "But we won't wait for long. We don't have all the time in the worlds to wait, you know."

The dwarf nods and dashes off-screen. As soon as we hear the sound of a door opening and closing, the Head looks at me with urgency in her eyes.

"J997, how is your hacking coming along?" asks the Head. "Have you had any success in determining their location?"

"Not yet," I say. "There is a powerful encryption that they use to hide their location from outsiders. I will do my best, but I cannot guarantee I will be able to break it in a timely fashion."

"You *have* to break it," says the Head. She reaches over to me and touches my shoulder with her other hand. "This is our only chance to strike a decisive blow against Reunification. At the very least, if our plan works, it will undoubtedly force them to delay their plans, which should give us more time to figure out how to defeat them permanently."

"Yes, I know," I say. "When the Founder appears on screen, try to keep him distracted for as long as possible. I believe I can break through the encryption, but I just need time."

"I will grant you as much time as I am able," says the Head. "But it won't be much, because we still need to rescue Kojama after this."

I nod in thanks and continue to focus on breaking the encryption. It is a complicated formula and very well designed, but I do not give up, because giving up is not an option.

A couple of minutes later, I am still trying to hack through the encryption, but then five beings—three of whom are probably Elders, though I do not know who the other two are—step into our view on the hologram. Four of them stand in the back, wearing cloaks that make it hard to determine their identities, especially since they are so out of focus on the hologram, but the fifth, a young Delanian woman with blonde hair and a small nose, steps into the forefront, looking at the Head without any fear.

"Who are you?" says the blonde woman to the Head.

The Head, however, ignores the question and says instead, "I wish to speak with the Founder, not you or the Elders."

The Head's brusqueness, however, does not deter the woman, who folds her arms over her chest and says, "Sorry, but I am Kiriah, the Leader of Reunification. Negotiating with enemies is one of my duties."

Without warning, Xacron-Ah begins gagging. He seems to be reacting to the sound of Kiriah's voice, because he is leaning forward in his chair and clearly trying to shout, although with the gag in his mouth, he only succeeds in sounding like he is dying. Lanresia immediately slaps him in the face with her gun, causing Xacron-Ah to go silent, although his good eye is still focused longingly on Kiriah's form on the hologram.

This is also the first time I see Kiriah. She does not look like a powerful or intimidating foe, but there is something in the way she stands and looks at the Head that makes me think she is more dangerous than she appears.

"I don't care what your duties are," says the Head. "My agents and I specifically kidnapped Xacron-Ah in order to secure a screen meeting with the Founder. Where is he?"

That is a lie, seeing as we actually kidnapped Xacron-Ah for completely different reasons. But as long as that lie diverts their attention from what we are *actually* doing, I see no reason to worry about it.

Instead, I focus more on breaking through the encryption, putting forth more effort than ever into solving it. Still, I also listen to the Head and the Leader's conversation, as I, too, wish to know what Reunification is doing.

"He's busy," says Kiriah, still not showing any fear. "But I can take a message for him, if you'd like."

The Head's brows furrow. "I am not an idiot, Kiriah. Whatever the Founder is doing can't be more important than talking to me."

"Actually, it is," says Kiriah. "Why don't you just tell us your name already? I don't even know who you are."

The Head puts on a convincing fake sigh of exasperation, and then says, "Fine. I'm the Head of the Foundation. I presume you've heard of me?"

Kiriah scratches her neck. She does not seem as stunned by that revelation as I expected her to be, but perhaps she is hiding it. Not that it matters; I am about halfway close to breaking the encryption, after which Kiriah will have to deal with a far more shocking, in an unpleasant way, revelation than the Head's identity.

"So you survived our attack on your Delanian base," says Kiriah. "Interesting. I thought for sure you had died."

"Did you honestly believe that I would die in that attack?" says the Head. "I guess, if you thought *that*, the Founder must not have told you very much about me, did he?"

Kiriah waves off the Head's words, saying, "That doesn't

matter. Where is Xacron-Ah? I don't see him."

"He's currently to my left, just off-screen," says the Head. "But I suppose it wouldn't do any harm to show him. J997, please bring our captive on screen."

Although I am still trying to break the encryption, I can still move around and obey her orders. Lanresia unties Xacron-Ah from his chair and I pull him up to his feet (although we keep his arms tied behind his back). I drag Xacron-Ah to the hologram, while Lanresia follows behind us, aiming her gun at Xacron-Ah's back to ensure that our captive does not try to make a break for it.

We allow Xacron-Ah to look at the hologram for only a moment before pulling him away at a nod from the Head. Xacron-Ah makes noises of protest, but they are barely audible through his gag and completely incomprehensible. Still, he doesn't resist when Lanresia and I drag him back to his chair and tie him back up, while the Head continues her conversation with Kiriah.

"So you see," says the Head, "we're not bluffing when we say that we have him. In fact, that is how we are contacting you at all. We are using his com-watch to connect with your computers, as you no doubt already know."

When we finish tying Xacron-Ah back up, I return my attention to breaking the encryption. I am a little over halfway done now, but I can tell that it will not be much longer before I break through entirely. As long as the Head keeps Kiriah and the other agents of Reunification distracted, I should be able to break through and get the knowledge we are looking for.

"Very well," says Kiriah. "I believe you. I can see that you have Xacron-Ah and will hurt him if you don't get what you want from us."

"More or less," says the Head. "Now that we have that out of the way, I demand to speak with the Founder. I don't care about small-fry like you or those three Elders behind your back. What I care about is talking to your true leader."

The Head can certainly sound as authoritative and commanding as a queen when she needs to. Of course, I know that she is a far more reasonable lady than she appears; even so, if I did not know her that well, I might have mistaken her for a cruel leader.

Wait … what's this? I sense that another system has connected to Xacron-Ah's com-watch. It does not try to stop me from breaking through the encryption—I am still essentially invisible to Reunification's computers—but that doesn't mean it has benevolent intentions for us. I pay careful attention to it, though that makes it harder to pay attention to the conversation between the Head and Kiriah at the same time.

"As I said before, he is not available," says Kiriah. "If you want to deal with us, you have to speak with me. It's not exactly a complicated concept for you to wrap your head around, you know."

Kiriah seems quite determined not to let the Head speak with the Founder. I wonder why that is, although I have no time to worry about that, because now I am starting to notice that this other computer is attempting to gain access to Xacron-Ah's files. I consider blocking it, but I am so focused on breaking the encryption that I decide it isn't worth it. Whatever Reunification's computers are trying to do is probably not important at the moment; besides, I cannot divide my attention any further than I have without decreasing my own efficiency.

The Head sighs heavily and says, "Fine. Although I wonder if the Founder simply does not want to talk to me because he doesn't want to see me again."

"And what does that mean?" says Kiriah. "Do you know the Founder?"

"We've met before," says the Head. "But that is irrelevant to the discussion. Let's start our deal."

'We've met before'—that reminds me of what Xacron-Ah told me earlier, about the Founder crying out about how he wishes his relationship with the mysterious 'Kara' was mended. Unless my audio receptors are malfunctioning, I catch a hint of disappointment in the Head's voice, mixed with disgust, although what that means, I do not know.

But again, that is not important, because I still have to focus my efforts on breaking the encryption. I am about 70% finished, but I still have a ways to go, so I keep at it.

"All right," says Kiriah. "What do you want from us?"

"Simple," says the Head. "In exchange for Xacron-Ah, I want you to cease all operations on both Dela and Xeeo. You will then disband Reunification and stop trying to reunite the two worlds."

The Head certainly does not mince words when it comes to making deals. She says that with a simple authoritative and doesn't even stutter. It is an effective psychological tactic, to be sure.

Then someone else—one of the Elders, the Checrom, although I do not know her name—speaks before Kiriah can so much as utter one word. "Utterly ridiculous. Xacron-Ah is a valuable agent, but he is not *that* valuable. We will not cease our operations on both worlds just to get one agent back."

I look at Xacron-Ah when she says that. He looks devastated, although I don't know why, seeing as he must have already known about how they all really feel about him. Maybe he used to think that the Elders appreciated him, but apparently that is not the case if this Elder's words are representative of the opinions of the rest.

"Are you certain?" says the Head. She smirks. "If that's your final answer, I suppose that's your right. As for us, we'll just take Xacron-Ah's personal files and distribute them to the Xeeonite and Delanian governments, which will of course reveal your existence and your plans to everyone, which I think would make it a great deal harder for you to complete your precious Mission, wouldn't you say?"

That is not something the Head mentioned we would do, but maybe her threat is only meant to fool them. After all, we are supposed to locate Reunification's base, not send Xacron-Ah's files to the governments of both worlds. I am not certain we can do so anyway, as that requires us having access to Xacron-Ah's files, which a quick scan shows are locked behind an encryption that looks too complicated and time-consuming for me to hack through at the moment.

Speaking of Xacron-Ah's files, I notice that the Reunification computer is still trying to access them. In fact, it may have already accessed them, but again, I only have enough time and energy to focus on one thing at a time, so I resume identifying the location of Reunification's base.

Kiriah steps forward, her eyes fixed squarely on the Head's face. "You wouldn't."

The Head shrugs. "I don't have any reason not to. While I

would prefer to keep our conflict a secret from the public, I also realize that Reunification is not equipped to deal with the combined might of the Xeeonite *and* Delanian governments, even if you have agents on the inside of both groups. I can't imagine that the United Federation of Xeeonite Nations or the Mystical Alliance of Dela would be happy to learn that you are trying to take both of their worlds out of existence."

Name-dropping the two largest international governmental alliances in both worlds—smart move, I must admit. Even on the hologram, I can see Kiriah's expression turning into a terrified frown. She might even be sweating, though that is hard to tell from here.

"So as you can see," says the Head, "it is obvious who has the power in this negotiation. If you agree to our demands, we will let Xacron-Ah go free. We might not even tell the authorities about your illegal activities on both worlds. Everyone can return to their normal lives without ever having to answer for their crimes."

That is the biggest lie the Head has said so far in this negotiation. I know for a fact that she has no intention whatsoever of letting anyone from Reunification get away with even the smallest crime, even in the unlikely event that they agree to our pretend demands.

Anyway, I've now chipped away at 80% of the encryption. Just a little bit more now.

"Well?" says the Head, after a short period of silence from Kiriah. "I am awaiting your answer, Kiriah. Either cease operations and hand the Founder over to us, or get ready to face the public."

Kiriah bites her lower lip. She looks off-screen for a moment before brushing her bangs off of her forehead and saying, in a flat voice, "So this is your deal, is it? Force us to end our operations or else expose us to the worlds, which would do the same thing, more or less."

"Exactly," says the Head. "Again, what is your answer? Will you accept it or reject it?"

As soon as the Head says that, Reunification's computer—the one that is trying to get access to Xacron-Ah's files—suddenly vanishes. It leaves so quickly that it catches my interest. I look and see that the encryption protecting Xacron-Ah's files has been broken, but there are no files beyond it. Strange. Why would anyone place an encryption on a folder that has no files in it?

But … what if there *were* files in it, but not anymore? Maybe the files have been deleted or removed. It is possible, but I do not know for certain.

At least, I don't know until Kiriah says, in a confident, even arrogant, voice, "Head, you didn't honestly expect us to fall for that, did you?"

The Head frowns in confusion. "What? What do you mean? This is not some trickery or deception on our part. We actually do have Xacron-Ah. You saw him yourself."

"I saw that," says Kiriah. "But you seem to think that you have us in a bind, when in truth, you don't."

"You're bluffing," says the Head. "I can see through your false confidence."

"False confidence?" says Kiriah. She gestures at herself. "This is all one hundred percent real here."

It is hard for me to tell how surprised and confused the Head really is. She seems genuinely surprised, but knowing her, she could just as easily be putting on an act. The Head is a difficult organic to read, for sure.

"I don't understand," says the Head. "There is clearly no way out of this situation that will end well for you. Though nice try with your attempt to convince me that your confidence is real; all I see is a weak attempt at bluffing."

"Believe what you want about my confidence, but the fact is, this is not as sticky a situation as you are trying to make it out to be," says Kiriah. She folds her arms over her chest again. "So you think that you can distribute Xacron-Ah's files to the public, thus revealing our existence to the worlds."

"Exactly," says the Head. "We have already established this. I don't see why you need to repeat it."

I do, but I do not say so aloud, because I am busy focusing on the encryption. I am almost there; 90% now. Not much longer before I finally get the coordinates of their location.

Meanwhile, Kiriah gestures at something off screen and one of the floating monitors I saw before flies over to her. She then gestures at the floating monitor and says, "Because I've already deleted those files from his com-watch."

The floating monitor turns to face us. The Head leans forward to get a better look at it in the hologram, and I also try to see it. Written on the monitor, in large red letters, are the words 'FILES DELETED.' There is no mistaking the meaning behind those words.

"But … how?" says the Head. "I did not even realize you were doing it."

I did, but I do not say that aloud. Better to let the Head handle this; anyway, I am now at 95%. Just a few more minutes and soon

I will crack it completely.

"Xacron-Ah's com-watch is connected to our headquarters' systems," says Kiriah, who sounds very proud of her 'victory' against us. "As a result, our computers have access to the files stored on it. While you talked, I had one of our computers go in and delete every last file on his com-watch. Now you have nothing to show to anyone and nothing to use against us."

The Head pulls back, looking defeated, although I suspect it's an act more than anything. "I … this can't be …"

"But it is," says Kiriah. She pats the floating monitor beside her. "You can see the proof for yourself on the monitor. Xac's com-watch is good only for contacting us now, but of course that is not what you need it for, right?"

The Head still appears defeated, while I hear Xacron-Ah grunt in approval behind us. I look at Lanresia; she does not seem as defeated as the Head, although even she appears to be affected by the Head's negative reaction.

I resume my focus on breaking the encryption: 99%. Just a few more seconds now.

"Now," says Kiriah, "I think we are done negotiating with you fools. We have some very important business to attend to, you see, and I just don't have the time to waste talking to a toothless tiger like you anymore."

As soon as Kiriah finishes speaking, I finally crack the encryption. I now have access to Reunification's location, but I do not dwell on this information. I instead gather it, format it into a simple text file, and send it to the Database immediately. I, of course, do so anonymously—so the Database does not track me down—but regardless, the deed is done.

Kiriah then raises her hand, perhaps to shut off the monitor, but before she does so, I say to the Head, in a louder voice so that everyone, both here and in the hologram, can hear me, "Head, I have ascertained the coordinates and location of Reunification's headquarters in the Dead Lands. I have now sent these coordinates to the Database, which the government of Xeeon will also receive shortly."

The Head smiles and then looks at me directly. "Thank you, J997. I appreciate the effort. Have you received a response yet?"

"None," I say. "But anonymous tips are rarely responded to. Most likely, the Database will send a squadron of J bots out to investigate the claim. Once they have determined that the claim has a basis in fact, I imagine they'll send an entire special forces team to take control of the base and arrest any Reunification agents they can find, maybe even a small army, because I made sure to include not only the base's location, but its size and number of residents, which was also included with the rest of its data."

"Wonderful," says the Head. She then turns to look at the members of Reunification again. "How did you like my acting? I tried to look as devastated as I could, in order to make you think that your little revelation had actually set us back. Of course it didn't. Because you see, Kiriah, I have decided to repay in kind for your slaughtering my agents. Let's see how long you last when the government of Xeeon decides to attack you."

Kiriah looks astonished by this turn of events. As for Xacron-Ah, he begins cursing; at least, I think he is, although it is hard to tell because of the gag in his mouth. I can guess what kind of curses he is speaking at us, however, because his sailor speak is well-known among the J bot law enforcers, even among ones like me, who have never served as his bodyguard before.

Then someone else steps forward into the hologram. He is a Delanian human with brown hair and a black cloak. He looks similar to Kiriah in appearance, which makes me wonder if they are related.

Whether they are or are not, he points directly at the Head's face and says, "Ye cur and wench, how dare ye do this! Ye are nothing but the scum of the earth, the dirt between the toes of the giants, a blight on the universe. Once I see ye in person, I will make ye wish that ye had never been born, ye monster."

His way of speaking is quite archaic. The mobile Database says that he is speaking a variant of the High Tongue, an ancient dialect spoken by many Delanians prior to King Waran-Una's rise to power. That makes me wonder why he still speaks it; then again, the mobile Database also says that the High Tongue is still spoken by a minority of Delanians who continue to worship the Old Gods, largely in defiance of Waran-Una's rule, which many of them see as unjust and even evil.

The Head does not seem offended by the man's archaic curses; instead, she smiles in amusement and says, "I've never been called a wench before, but it doesn't really matter. Soon, all of you will be behind bars or hiding in the dirt like the rats you are. Meanwhile, we will be sitting here, laughing at your agony. Tell the Founder I said hello."

She then shuts off the hologram with a tap of the com-watch's screen before any of the Reunification agents can respond. She turns to face us, a satisfied smile on her face as she folds her arms over her chest.

"Now, then," says the Head, "why don't we get started on rescuing Kojama? We have no time to lose, because his execution is still on schedule."

I nod and say, "Agreed. I will find Konoa and then we can place my AI in your Third Eye chip. How long will that take?"

"Not long at all," says the Head. "Even though we don't exactly have the best or most advanced tools available to us, I believe we can still transfer your AI into the Third Eye and then place the chip inside Konoa in a short amount of time."

"All right," I say. "Then I will go find Konoa and we can begin the process."

Chapter 5

It is not long before the Head, Konoa, and I are in the first floor living room of our current headquarters. The wallpaper is peeling, there are some holes in the ceiling, and a tiny mouse scurries across the floor into the hole; nonetheless, there is enough room in this place for us all to stand in.

Though not all of us will be standing. The Head has me lie on the moth-eaten sofa in the center of the room. She then has Konoa bring in her computer, to which she attaches the Third Eye chip. She then pulls out a folded up cable, which she attaches to a port on the computer's hard drive before turning it on.

I frown when I see her work. "A cable? That seems primitive. Why not use a wireless transfer? Wouldn't that be easier and more efficient than using a cable?"

"We do not, unfortunately, have access to that level of technology at the moment," says the Head with a sigh. "We could possibly return to the ruins of our base in the Dead Lands and attempt to salvage what we can find, but that is too risky because of the possibility that Reunification may be watching the base to make sure we don't return. Better to make do with what we have found in this building and in the surrounding neighborhood in general." She pauses, and then asks, "You J bots do have ports for cables, yes?"

"Yes we do," I say. "While we J bots typically use wireless communication with other computers, we do have ports for cables built into our bodies, as we sometimes run into old technology in our line of work that sometimes holds valuable evidence we need to solve a crime."

"Is your body compatible with a B-90X cable?" asks the Head, holding up the cable she hooks up to the computer.

I nod. "Yes. We are compatible with anything above B-89Z. We cannot hook up with cables older than that, however."

"Lucky us, because we just happen to have a B-90X cable on hand," says the Head. She looks over my body briefly and then frowns. "I don't see the port for me to plug this into."

"I will show it to you soon enough," I say. "But I first want to know what will happen if the Third Eye is destroyed."

The Head laughs. "That won't happen. It will be inside Konoa's body, safe from all harm. You don't need to worry about that."

"But if it does happen," I say, "then what? Will my AI be destroyed as well?"

The Head does not look like she wants to answer that question, but then nods reluctantly and says, "Yes, it will be. There's no way for this chip to return your AI to your body in the event it is destroyed. And if the Third Eye is damaged, then your AI will be damaged as well."

"But even that may not be a problem, if you think about it," Konoa says. He gestures at me. "We can duplicate his personality, make a backup that we can keep here. That way, should something happen to the Third Eye, then we will still have J997, right? At least we won't lose him."

107

"It is not that simple, Konoa," I say. I gesture at my head. "We J bots are operated by a highly complicated personality program informally called the Homunculus. The Homunculus is what gives us our apparent personalities and ability to store memories. Each Homunculus is unique and impossible to remake in the event it is destroyed; my Homunculus, in other words, is what gives me my individuality."

"So are you saying we cannot backup your personality onto another server or hard drive?" says the Head.

I nod. "Exactly. The files that constitute our personalities and memories are too large and complicated to be transferred over onto an ordinary server or hard drive. The Database is the only computer system in Xeeo that can hold a Homunculus. And it does in fact keep a copy of each Homunculus stored on its hard drive for safekeeping; even so, the Database has at least one hundred servers dedicated to the Homunculus copies alone."

"If your Homunculus is destroyed, then does that mean you are truly dead?" says the Head.

"We J bots cannot really 'die' in the sense that organics can," I say. "But yes, if my Homunculus is destroyed, I would indeed be gone forever."

"And we can't duplicate you?" says the Head. "Not even for a backup copy that we could upload to your original body in the event of your death?"

"You would need at least one thousand terabytes just to store it," I say. "Besides, it is illegal for someone outside of the force to duplicate the personality of a J bot, and we have already broken more laws than I am comfortable with breaking at the moment."

"You sound very calm about all of this," the Head observes.

"Are you certain that you are all right?"

"I lack emotions of any sort," I say. "This may be akin to discussing your death to you humans, but to me, it is no more controversial or uncomfortable than discussing the weather."

Both the Head and Konoa look displeased at my words. I wonder if I should make another joke to make them feel better. It is true that none of my jokes ever make them laugh, but maybe this time I will get 'lucky,' as the comedians put it, and they will find my jokes humorous.

"Think of it this way," I say. "My body will still be here, even if I die. Getting upset over my 'death' would be like a dog getting upset that it is a dog; it simply makes no sense."

The two of them look at me like I have lost my mind. I sigh and say, "It is a joke. An original joke I came up with on my own, in fact."

"Well, it wasn't very funny," says the Head. "At all."

"Oh," I say. "Well, then I will simply have to try harder. Maybe one of these days, I will finally tell a joke that will get people to laugh."

The Head's skeptical look tells me that she has written me off as a lost cause, but that is fine, because I am not trying to make her specifically laugh anyway. I make a mental note of doing a more in-depth study of *Secrets of Humor* later; maybe if I do, I will then learn how to tell a funny joke.

Konoa bites his lower lip. "Well, if your Homunculus is too large to fit inside an ordinary server or hard drive, how do you intend to fit in the Third Eye? It wasn't designed with J bots in mind, so I doubt it is large enough to hold your personality."

"True, but there is some way I can do it," I say. I rub my

forehead. "We J bots can create compressed versions of our personality files that can be transferred onto other, smaller hard drives and servers. These compressed files are generally temporary, however, and lack much of the complexity and functionality of the full version."

"What does that mean?" says Konoa, tilting his head in confusion.

"Well, it simplifies my thinking, for one," I say. "I cannot come up with very complex plans or ideas. I am still recognizably me, of course, and retain most of my memories, but I am much simpler than I normally am. In addition, I do not have any connection to the Database or the mobile Database, which means I have far less information and knowledge with which to work. I do not especially prefer the compressed version of my files, which I have had to work with before, because it is never quite as effective as my full personality."

"I don't like the idea of having a simpler J997 on hand," says Konoa, looking at the Head as he says that. "Especially since we are attempting to break into the most well-protected prison in the world. What if we get stuck in a tight situation that requires a complex plan?"

"I can still be of use in my compressed form," I say. "While I do not have access to the Database, my compressed form does allow me to choose which files in the mobile Database to copy and take with me and which to leave. I can download all of the files on the Xeeon City Prison into my compressed form, which I can then share with you so we can use them to rescue Kojama."

"Well, I see no reason why we shouldn't use his compressed form, then," says the Head. "It's not like we have much time to sit around and discuss this, anyway. Every minute we waste here is another minute that could be spent rescuing Kojama."

Konoa still does not look pleased by this turn of events, but he stops protesting anyway. He simply steps aside as my B-90X port flings open on my chest, allowing the Head to hook me up to her computer without any fuss.

"There," says the Head, standing back up to her full height and turning her attention back to her computer. "Now, let's begin the process of uploading your compressed personality to the Third Eye. Ready, J997?"

I nod. "I will turn myself off in the meantime. These types of file transfers are usually easier and quicker when I am inactive, but I will reactivate as soon as I am inside Konoa's body."

"Very good," says the Head. She places her fingers on the keyboard and begins typing away. "Begin file transfer ... now."

As soon as she says that, I shut my body down while simultaneously generating the compressed version of my personality. The last thing I see, before my optics shut off, is the glow of the computer's monitor on the Head's face and Konoa's own uncertain gaze.

REBOOTING ... COMPRESSED FILES VALID AND COMPLETE. REACTIVATING UNIT J997 AI.

When I open my optics again, I see my own robotic body lying on the moth-eaten sofa, the arms folded over the stomach. That is my body. It is lying there, looking almost like a corpse, but I know it is still as functional as ever. It simply lacks my personality at the moment.

J997? says a voice I at first do not recognize. *Is that you?*

It takes me a minute to match the voice with one of the voice files in my compressed memory. It is the voice of Konoa, who sounds concerned and cautious, like he is approaching a dangerous wild animal. The caution seems unnecessary to me, considering he knows me already.

Anyway, yes, Konoa, it is me, J997. Where are you?

You are in my head, says Konoa. I then see an organic hand rise in front of my eyesight. *Can you see what I can see?*

Yes, I can. Is that your hand?

Yes, says Konoa. *What else can you see?*

Everything you can. My body, the sofa, and the floor. Why?

I just wanted to make sure that you and I can see the same things, says Konoa. *If you are going to be in my head like this, then it only makes sense that we know the limits of the Third Eye, right?*

I agree. I wish we had more time to perform more experiments to find out its exact limits, though.

Yeah, but we barely even have time for this conversation, much less time to mess around with it, Konoa says. *Anyway, how do you feel? Are you in pain?*

I cannot feel pain at all. How long have I been out?

Less than half an hour, if even that, says Konoa. *I was also out because the Head was putting the Third Eye inside me. It was a quick job, but god did my head hurt at first.*

I assume you are better now?

Yeah, says Konoa. *I can't even feel the chip in my brain anymore. Might as well not be there at all.*

"Konoa?" says the Head's voice, causing us to look to our left, where the Head is staring at us. "Is J997 activated yet?"

Seeing things from Konoa's point of view is … interesting. While his eyesight is quite good, it is not as clear or as crisp as my own optics. I cannot see as much detail as I normally do. That is not good, because it is sometimes the smallest details that can have the largest consequences.

"Yes," says Konoa. "He is. I just spoke with him now."

"Good," says the Head. "That means that the Third Eye works. I wish the engineers who designed it were still alive; then I could tell them that all of their hard work has finally paid off."

"What's our next plan of action?" says Konoa. "Where do we go from here?"

"To the Prison," says the Head. "You and J997 must break into it and rescue Kojama. Does J997 have the files on the Xeeo City Prison in his memory banks?"

"Yes, he does," says Konoa. He taps the side of his head. "Right up here, along with the rest of his memories."

"Excellent," says the Head. "Now, Konoa, you and J997 need to leave right away. Xacron-Ah said that Kojama's execution is for this morning; if you leave now, you might be able to make it to the prison in time to save him."

Konoa nods. "Yes, ma'am. We'll be back with Kojama in tow before you know it. Right, J997?"

Yes. We should have no trouble breaking in and saving Kojama, especially with the Database no doubt already sending out officers to Reunification's base in the Dead Lands.

"Then what are we waiting for?" says the Head. She gestures at the doorway behind her. "You two must go. And quickly, before the execution starts."

113

Before we leave the headquarters, Lanresia sees us off. She and Konoa kiss, which gives me a much closer look at her face than I like, but only for a brief moment. They then exchange words of good bye, although I pay little attention to it because their farewell is so inane and has nothing to do with me.

After that, Konoa steps outside of the abandoned apartment building and closes the door behind him. Konoa is quite regretful at leaving Lanresia behind, even though he knows it is for the best. I say nothing about it, seeing as I doubt he is in the mood to listen to any of my jokes at the moment.

All right, J997, says Konoa as he pulls the skull mask over his face again. *Which way do we go to get to the Prison?*

To the north.

Just straight north? Konoa says.

Yes. As long as you head in that direction, we should find the prison before the execution starts

What about security? Konoa asks. *Won't the guards notice me?*

Didn't Lanresia give you her concealment ring? That would help us avoid being seen.

No, Konoa says, shaking his head. *I'm not much of a wizard. I've always been more into technology, so even if she had given me the ring, it's not like I could have used it.*

That does pose a problem to us, but I believe we will be able to avoid detection from the J bots if we are smart.

You just tell me what to do and I'll listen, says Konoa. *Anyway, we can plan on the way there. For now, we must head north.*

Konoa dashes down the front steps of the abandoned

apartment building onto the empty streets in front of us. He then makes his way to the north, running as fast as he can, while at the same time keeping to the shadows and alleyways where no one can see us easily. He moves surprisingly quickly, like he has spent his whole life out here in the streets.

I actually did grow up here in Xeeon, Konoa says as he dashes through the streets. *My brothers and I grew up playing in these same streets, in fact. I only went to Dela after I joined the Foundation because the Head thought that I might be useful there.*

I see. Why did you join the Foundation in the first place?

Konoa does not answer at first, mostly because his attention is on our environment. He jumps over an overturned trash can and, when he lands on the street, he scares away some nearby rats, which crawl into a pile of garbage left behind by a trash company that is apparently not doing its job.

Finally, Konoa says, *I joined the Foundation because I wanted to get out of that grinding poverty that I was born into. It's not easy, getting out of poverty in Xeeon, so when the Foundation offered me a job, I took it. I'm still not exactly rich; however, I no longer have to worry about where my next meal is coming from (or didn't, before Reunification attacked), and I also have met the woman I love, so I see it as one of the best decisions I have ever made in my life.*

Konoa stops and jumps into another alleyway as a lone J bot flies overhead. When we look up to watch it pass, I recognize it as J347, although it flies by too fast for me to be certain.

So if you grew up in poverty, how did you learn how to work on J bots? Certified J bot technicians have to go to a qualified trade school, which are rather expensive due to how few trade schools have been approved by the Xeeon City Government to teach that particular skill.

Picked up a little bit here, a little bit there, Konoa says, peeking out from the alley to make sure no one else is going to be coming down this way. *What I'd do, as a kid, was find all kinds of old or abandoned or broken machines and take them apart and figure out how they worked. Sometimes I even figured out how to fix them, but most of the time, I didn't. I managed to get my hands on a few decommissioned J bots, which taught me a lot about how J bots work. When I joined the Foundation, I was given access to better technology, which is where I learned most of what I know today about robots like yourself.*

I cannot say I approve of your taking apart some of my fellow J bots in order to learn how we work. It is an illegal act that can earn you up to a decade in prison, plus a fine of 10,000 digits.

Konoa chuckles. *I don't really care, as you can probably guess. Anyway, you aren't seriously going to turn me in, are you? Not when we have to work together to save Kojama?*

I will not, partly because I agree that there are more urgent matters to attend to at the moment, and partly because I cannot even connect with the Database in this form anyway to inform it of your criminal acts. Besides, rescuing Kojama is a more urgent matter for us at the moment.

Sounds good to me, says Konoa. *As long as you tell me everything about Xeeon City Prison, I'll be happy. Anyway, all of this conversation is distracting me. Why don't you keep quiet until we reach the prison? Then we can continue talking there. You just take this time to think of a plan we can use to break in.*

116

RETALIATION

Okay. I believe more in focusing on the mission at hand than on any trivial conversation we may have anyway. Still, I appreciate you telling me a little about yourself. I can trust you better now than before.

Konoa smiles. *That's good to hear. Now let's go. Time's a-wasting.*

It takes us less than twenty minutes to reach Xeeon City Prison, which is quicker than I expected. Of course, we had the winning combination of Konoa's speed and agility plus my detailed knowledge of the city's shortcuts and back streets to help us shorten the journey.

When we arrive, the sky above is still quite dark, but with all of the city lights on, it almost looks like it is daytime. We hide in an alleyway between two buildings that are near the prison's walls, which cloaks Konoa in their shadow, allowing us to see the prison itself without fear of being spotted by the guards or security cameras on the outer walls.

Through Konoa's eyes, I see Xeeon City Prison's tall, thick concrete and metal walls, which, while not as big as the skyscrapers around us, are still an impressive size. Along the walls are J bots—more heavily armored than most, due to their jobs as prison wardens—patrolling the walls, while others fly above to provide air support for their ground-based companions. There are few citizens on the streets around the Prison, which is intentional, because most Xeeonian citizens typically avoid this part of the city due to the ruthless reputation of the guards, which has been known on occasion to be extended to suspicious citizens who got too close to the Prison's walls for the guards' liking.

Our position allows us to see the entrance, which is a massive set of metal gates that appear nigh-impossible to knock down or break through. They are guarded by a dozen J bots, but there are usually much more than that, which makes me wonder if the Database has taken some of the exterior guards and sent them to the Dead Lands in response to our anonymous call. If so, that will make this rescue mission a lot easier for us.

All right, J997, Konoa says, his eyes focused firmly on the walls of the prison. *What are we up against, exactly?*

Four hundred and fifty guards, though only half of them are active at any one time, because they often rotate with their counterparts who are part of the active force that patrols the streets. It is rarely necessary for all of them to be present here at the same time.

So we have two hundred and twenty-five guards to deal with, then? Konoa says.

Essentially, yes. Most of them are on the inside, where they are needed to keep the prisoners in line. But they are not the only security hazards we must watch out for.

What are the others?

The Prison itself is a security hazard. It is connected with the Database and has built-in security features, such as drones that can be used to chase after escapees or mechanical limbs that can pop out of the floors, walls, or ceiling to recapture or delay escapees. Various tricks and traps also exist, such as floors that fall away to reveal a deep pit with unclimbable walls, and thick, sharp metal netting that can be dropped from the ceiling onto prisoners. The Prison is capable of making these decisions consciously, similar to how we J bots behave.

Konoa gulps. *So the Prison is essentially 'alive,' just like you?*

In a way, yes. Its AI, which we call the Brain, is not as sophisticated as mine, but it is intelligent enough to retain most escapees and cannot be easily fooled or reasoned with. Its single-minded determination is what makes it a threat, because it will not stop trying to capture you until it succeeds in doing so. It is why no one has ever escaped from Xeeon City Prison before. The guards are a 'walk in the park,' as you humans might say, in comparison to the Prison itself.

But there must be some way to get past it, Konoa says. *Right?*

There is. We can bypass most of its features by traveling through the sewers underneath it. We can then find another way into the prison without being noticed.

You mean the sewers are connected to the prison? Konoa says. *Like how you and Lanresia used the sewers to enter the Mayor's Mansion?*

Similar, but not exactly the same. Unlike the Mayor's Mansion, Xeeon City Prison has no secret exit, mostly because if there was one, it would be too easy for the prisoners to use to escape or for their friends on the outside to use to spring them. Still, I do know that the sewers connect with the prison's power supply, so we might be able to turn off the power long enough for us to enter the prison and rescue Kojama.

If you say so, Konoa says. *But what about the guards? They are clearly not connected to the prison's power grid. Even if we successfully managed to knock out its power long enough for us to rescue Kojama, we would still have to make it past the J bot guards.*

True. The guards will no doubt become even more vigilant if we manage to shut off the power. They will then send someone to

119

check on it and probably restore the power, assuming the backup power generators do not kick on once the power goes out. It is possible, however, that the guards might be too distracted by the prisoners' attempts to escape from the depowered Prison to send someone down to check on the power grid, but that is not very likely.

I am starting to think that we did not think this plan through as well as we could have, Konoa says. He scratches the back of his neck. *Freeing Kojama doesn't seem quite as doable as it did earlier, when we were in the safety of our temporary headquarters.*

It is a difficult task indeed. But I believe we can do it. As I said, our main problem is dealing with the Prison itself. Even if all of the guards leave, the Prison has more than enough automated security features by itself to keep inmates from escaping. The Prison is actually designed to be able to keep the prisoners behind bars by itself in the unlikely event that there are no guards to help.

Seems to me we need to figure out a way to knock out the Brain, then, says Konoa. *How many backup generators does it have, anyway?*

One hundred, according to the files on the Prison that I downloaded from the mobile Database.

Konoa groans. *One hundred? You aren't telling me another bad joke, are you?*

I said that Xeeon City Prison is the best prison in the world. Did you think I am exaggerating?

Well, I'm not sure what we're supposed to do, then, says Konoa. He glances at his com-watch. *Not long now before Kojama's execution, if my com-watch is accurate. I don't see how we are going to be able to rescue Kojama unless you happen to have any suggestions you haven't mentioned yet.*

Give me a few minutes to think. This is indeed a complex problem, but I think I can figure it out if I have a little bit of time in which to think it over.

All right, Konoa says. *But don't take long, because, like I said, we don't have much time.*

I consider our situation. The Xeeon City Prison has many defenses and layers to it. It is by no means impossible to break into or out of, but it has been designed—and so far has proven—to be impossible for its inmates to escape from. It is the Brain that is the most troublesome aspect. Because, while it is not as sophisticated as J bot AI, the Brain is still very effective at making sure no one can break into or out of it on its watch.

And, as Konoa and I have already discussed, simply knocking out its power grid will not work. The prison has too many backup generators to restore power in the event that its main grid fails; it would be a temporary measure at best.

If only the Brain was on our side, then it would be easier to get around. If the Brain wanted to help us and not harm us, then rescuing Kojama would be exceptionally easy.

That is when a new plan occurs to me. It is a little odd, but when I think about it, it seems like the best plan we can use, given the current situation.

Konoa, I have a plan.

What is it? Konoa asks. *I'm all ears.*

You need to find the central computer system containing the Brain and insert the Third Eye into it. That will then allow me to override the Brain's control of the Prison, which will allow me to rescue Kojama easily.

My connection to Konoa helps me sense how uneasy that plan makes him. *Uh, are you sure about that? Sounds dangerous.*

It is a simple matter that should work if we do it right. The Brain's AI and J bot AI are similar enough that I should be able to assume command of the prison without too much difficulty. I also understand the defenses programmed into the Brain by its programmers to prevent it from being hacked by outsiders, so overcoming whatever resistance it may show toward me should not take long.

What I'm more concerned about is leaving you behind, says Konoa. *How are we supposed to retrieve your AI if you become the Prison's new AI? You yourself said this is the only copy of yourself.*

That is a good point, Konoa, but I will be fine. The important thing is that you need to rescue Kojama, and this is the best way to go about doing it, in my opinion.

You mean you aren't afraid of being found out and captured? Konoa says. *Because it sure seems to me like a good way to be captured and your memory dissected. I hope you didn't forget at this point what your fellow J bots think about you.*

It is fine. You can just come and pick me up after we rescue Kojama. Worse comes to worse, I can always send my AI through the net into my old body. It should not be much of a problem for me.

I just don't like the idea of leaving you, with all of your knowledge and memories of the Foundation, here, where you will undoubtedly be caught and dissected once they realize who you are, says Konoa. *That's a huge security risk for the Foundation no matter how you look at it, even if you somehow manage to transfer your AI back to your old body.*

I agree, but we really have very little time to come up with another plan that will not leave me at the mercy of my former allies. This is the only way I know of that will allow us to complete the mission.

But how am I even supposed to remove you from my brain? Konoa asks. He taps his forehead. *I'm not exactly a master surgeon, you know. Seems to me that you are stuck up there.*

No, I am not, actually. I have done a quick scan of the Third Eye and have discovered that it can actually remove itself from the brain and move on its own. It is an ingenious little device, which makes me wonder at the technological prowess of the programmers who designed it.

So you can leave on your own, then, says Konoa. *Okay, but that doesn't change the fact that there is no possible way I can get you into the Prison's systems. I mean, I would need direct access to the Prison's central mainframe to do that, wouldn't I? I'd imagine that that is pretty well-guarded, for obvious reasons.*

I know how to reach it, even how to bypass its defenses. All you need to do is follow my directions and we should find the computer's mainframe with little trouble.

Sounds too easy, says Konoa. *I don't trust things that sound too easy.*

I did not say it will be easy. I just said that we can find its mainframe with little trouble. That does not describe how difficult it may be for us to actually access the Brain. I hope you understand the difference.

Sort of, Konoa admits. *It seems to me that we have a big task ahead of ourselves no matter how you look at it.*

Is that any reason to give up, though? We already face many difficult tasks, not the least of which is stopping Reunification's plan to reunite the worlds, which will result in countless deaths if it is not stopped. This is a walk in the park in comparison to that.

I know, Konoa says. *I just wish we could come up with a better plan, one that* didn't *involve leaving you behind to be captured by the J bots.*

Life is not always the way we would like it to be, Konoa. Besides, my fellow J bots are not as bad as Reunification; even if they capture me, they will not be cruel. I can assure you of that.

Can you assure me that they won't download your memory onto the Database and reveal all of our secrets to the worlds? Konoa asks.

I cannot guarantee that, although as this is my compressed form, I do not have as complete a memory as I normally would. That is to say, the secrets I do know about the Foundation at the moment are minimal at best. And again, I can still escape through the net if necessary, though that would mean leaving behind the Third Eye.

You still know some of our secrets, though, if not most, Konoa says. *But I guess you're right. Yours is the only workable plan we have at the moment, so just give me the directions to the Prison's mainframe and I will head there right away.*

All right. We must first head under the sewers, because the mainframe is located under the streets. I will give you further instructions as we head down there.

All right, Konoa says. *Down we go, then.*

RETALIATION

We head down into the sewers, which reminds me of earlier, when Lanresia and I kidnapped Xacron-Ah. Only this time, when Konoa climbs down the ladder and looks around, we see no sign of the lizard humanoids from before, although that does not mean they are not here, perhaps hiding in the water or in the shadows. Of course, it seems unlikely that there are any down here, seeing as those lizard humanoids in Xacron-Ah's emergency exit had, in all likelihood, been placed there to protect Xacron-Ah specifically; still, it is better to be safe than sorry, so we advance into the sewers with more caution than usual.

The files about the city's layout show that the Prison is connected to the sewers, for reasons that are quite obvious. What most people do not know, however, is that the Xeeon City Prison's mainframe is also located near the sewers. This may seem like an odd design choice—building a complex computer system near a sewer system, to the point where you can actually access the computer system's room from these sewers—but in truth, it is not as illogical as it seems.

What Konoa and I are looking for is the maintenance tunnel for the mainframe. It is in the sewers due to the ease of access that the sewers provide workers; however, that does not mean that it will be easy to access once we find it. The maintenance still has many defenses to keep out hackers and potential intruders; in fact, some say that the mainframe has even more defenses than the Prison itself, although that is largely hyperbole spread by prison inmates and criminals, as well as by J bots in an attempt to discourage anyone from doing what Konoa and I are planning to do. Despite the rumors, however, it is a fact that it is well-defended, though my knowledge of its security systems should allow us to make short work of its defenses.

With my instructions, Konoa and I soon discover the entrance to the maintenance tunnel after only five minutes of searching, which is a plain, locked metal door that has no handles or doorknobs. Nor will it simply slide open on its own; in order for it to open, we must input the unlock password on the hidden keypad, which we find flipped into the wall to the door's right. Konoa presses his hand against the portion of the wall where the keypad is hidden, causing the keypad to flip open with ease.

All right, Konoa says, his fingers hovering over the small keypad. *What's the password?*

The password is 'kajon,' a Xeeonite word meaning 'bread,' though I'm sure you know that already, seeing as you are a native of Xeeo yourself.

Bread?

The password is not meant to be easily guessed. Because bread has nothing to do with the Prison or the Brain, that means it should be harder for hackers to guess. It is not even spelled correctly, but that's irrelevant at the moment. Just input the password and we should be able to get inside with little trouble.

If you say so, Konoa says as he types the password into the keypad, although he hardly sounds enthusiastic about it.

Once Konoa finishes inputting the password, he presses the 'enter' key and the thick metal door before us slides open without a sound. We look both ways down the sewers, just to make sure no one is following us, before we step into the maintenance tunnel and the door closes behind us.

It is not too dark down here. The maintenance tunnel has lights running along the edges of the ceiling, which allow us to see where we are going. Wiring and pipes running along the walls cover them almost completely. Some of the wiring crosses our path, while other wiring crawls over the ceiling above our heads. It creates a very claustrophobic environment; in fact, that is exactly how Konoa feels, but he does not allow his claustrophobic feelings to make him run away. He simply walks forward, albeit with more caution than usual.

Hey, Konoa says, gesturing at the wiring on the walls, floor, and ceiling. *Why don't I just cut these wires? That will probably knock out the power and the Brain long enough for us to get into the prison and free Kojama. Kojama might even be able to escape on his own; he's a pretty smart guy, after all, and if he's given the chance, he could do it, I'm sure.*

No. Knocking out the power will release all of the other prisoners in there, too. And trust me when I say that they are all much, much worse than Kojama could ever be. There is a reason that this prison has the strictest security of any prison in Xeeon or in the two worlds, and it is not because we felt like making it that way.

Okay, okay, says Konoa. *I get it.*

I do not think you do. Cutting the power down here would only lead to J bots being sent to investigate. They will then see and arrest us. No, it's better for us to go with our original plan; besides, I don't want to render moot all of the hard work that my fellow J bots put into arresting those criminals and putting them behind bars. I am fine with rescuing one 'criminal,' who clearly did not do anything to deserve such a title, but the others are all guilty and deserve to remain behind bars to serve whatever sentences that the Xeeon city court system handed down to them.

I guess you're right, says Konoa. *Sure would be simpler to knock out the Brain long enough for us to sneak in and rescue Kojama, though.*

Perhaps it would, but I also think it would be riskier. Although when I think about it, no matter what we do, we risk attracting the J bots' attention. And if they find and arrest us, they will likely jail us in the very Prison we are trying to break into.

Very true, says Konoa, although I sense a hint of disagreement in his tone, like he still thinks that knocking out the Brain briefly is a good idea. *Anyway, are there any security hazards down here that I should watch out for? Just seems unlikely to me that they would leave the maintenance tunnel unprotected like this.*

That's not as unlikely as you think. The maintenance tunnel is supposed to be easily accessed by the maintenance crew. Setting up a heavy, elaborate, and overly-complicated security system down here would only hurt, rather than help, the maintenance crew. After all, no one else outside of the J bots and the city's maintenance crews even know of this tunnel's location. Don't let your guard down, however, because there is still some security, albeit not as much.

Then what do I have to look out for? Konoa says. *You still haven't been entirely clear on that.*

Lasers, for one. Not the kind that will stun you or poke a hole through your brain, but security lasers that, if tripped, will place you inside a cage and send a message to the Database informing it of a break-in and requesting officers to apprehend the infiltrator. The lasers are invisible, by the way, so avoiding them is not easy.

Konoa stops and puts his hands on his hips. *How am I supposed to avoid tripping them if they are invisible? You're not making any sense.*

I will tell you where they are. My files on the Prison's security systems tell me the locations of each security laser. You won't have to worry about tripping them now, because I will let you know where they are before we run into them.

All right, says Konoa. *I'm listening, so tell me when you see any.*

Okay. There is one directly ahead of you, and another about five feet down after that. You can walk over the one ahead of you, but the one five feet down needs to be crawled under. And about a dozen yards beyond that are three lasers crisscrossing each other, but you can also get by that by crawling along the floor of the tunnel.

I give Konoa this kind of information the deeper we go into the maintenance tunnel. Due to the security lasers, this makes our trip down here much more time-consuming than it ordinarily would be; however, it also keeps us from being detected by the J bots, so I feel that this is justified.

In about ten minutes, we reach the end of the maintenance tunnel. Before us is a tall ladder that goes up into the darkness above, the only light being a red light that signals the exit.

Climb this ladder and we will reach the mainframe's room, I say. *This will take us directly underneath the Prison, but don't worry, because as long as we are smart and do this correctly, we should be fine.*

Konoa begins climbing up the ladder rung by rung. He moves quickly and without hesitation, because there isn't much time left before Kojama's execution starts, and soon we reach the hatch. Konoa bangs one fist against it, creating an echoing, metallic sound throughout the tunnel, but we do not hear anything else on the other side.

All right, J997, Konoa says. *How do we open this hatch?*

There should be another keypad in the shadows somewhere directly to your left. Password is 'extempus,' a Rathonian slang term meaning 'cookie.'

Konoa reaches out and feels a smooth keypad to his left, which he immediately begins typing on despite being unable to see the keys. *Is it me or does whoever came up with these passwords like baked goods?*

It's definitely not you, but I do not know the identity of whoever created these passwords, so I cannot help you there.

Right, says Konoa as he finishes typing in the password. *Well, it doesn't really matter all that much. Either way, we're going to get in and rescue Kojama, and that's all that matters.*

Once Kojama enters the password, the hatch lifts up automatically. We wait a couple of seconds to let the hatch rise enough for us to exit, and when it does, Konoa climbs out of the maintenance tunnel and onto the solid concrete floor of the mainframe's chamber. We then look around the room we have entered, our eyes darting about.

We have now entered the room housing the Brain's mainframe. It is a veritable mess of wires, piping, computer monitors, and servers humming and running at all times. The gigantic screens display video of the interior of the Prison; prisoners sitting in cells, guards patrolling the hallways, new prisoners being taken to their cells, and many other things besides, including video of the streets outside the walls. There are too many screens for us to focus on any one of them for very long, but we do not need to, because that is not what we came here to do.

All right, J997, Konoa says, looking around the massive room. *What are we looking for and where can I find it?*

The mainframe itself is in the center of the room. Just keep walking forward; it's not difficult to get to and there shouldn't be any security hazards in our way. Just be aware that the Brain might be watching us.

Konoa stops cold where he is. *Does that mean that the Brain will try to stop us?*

Unlikely. It will probably just assume that we are members of the maintenance crew coming down to check up on things. If it attempts to scan us, it will probably discover me and not try to get rid of us, seeing as I am a J bot and the Brain trusts us more than anyone else. We are safe as long as we do not cause any disturbances in here.

Then I guess we won't be safe for much longer, seeing as we're going to be causing quite a few disturbances very soon, Konoa says.

We advance deeper into the room, past the dozens of scenes playing out on the screens, past the large servers and pipes that make loud humming noises, toward a massive central computer at the very center of the Brain. This computer towers over everything else in the room, and is what all of the piping and wires are connected to. It is even vaguely shaped like a human brain; hence the name.

A red light blinks above the monitor of the gigantic computer before us. There is no keypad of any sort, because this mega computer is not designed to be used by organics. There is, however, a closed panel that can be flipped open labeled 'MAINTENANCE' that is unlocked.

Don't tell me that that's what we're looking for, says Konoa, stopping in front of the gigantic computer and staring at the labeled panel.

But that *is* what we are looking for. I would think that would make you happy, seeing as it didn't take us long to find it.

It just seems a little too *easy,* Konoa says. *Like someone is playing us.*

I know of no one who is playing us, Konoa. Sometimes, life is just that simple. I see no reason to over-think it. Besides, the files on the Xeeon City Prison don't indicate that there is anything to worry about here. We just need to flip open the panel and install the Third Eye into the Brain's mainframe. Then I will be able to take control of the Prison and free Kojama. Very simple.

If you say so, Kojama says as he reaches for the panel.

Just as he is about to flip the panel open, however, the loud sound of metal clanging shut causes us to look over his shoulder.

The hatch is closed, but we did not close it. Not only that, but a *click*—audible even over the humming of the servers and the banging pipes—indicates that it is locked again. Of course, we can open it from the outside if necessary, but the fact that it locked all on its own is troubling, to put it lightly.

"Uh oh," says Konoa, actually saying those words aloud. "Why did the hatch close and lock itself on its own when there's no one in here with us?"

"That is because you are not alone," says a metallic voice from the computer in front of us. "Because you are with me."

Metal tentacles suddenly shoot down from the wires above

and wrap around Konoa's arms. The tentacles lift Konoa off the ground even as he kicks and struggles against them, but all of his resistance and struggle does nothing to save us as we are raised higher and higher into the air.

"Resistance is futile," says the voice again, this time sounding like it is coming from the entire room. "You must not be allowed to escape for your crimes. I have already sent a message to the J bots to come here quickly and arrest you for breaking into the Brain."

"Let me go!" Konoa shouts. "Right now, or I'll—"

"Your threats do not frighten me," says the voice of the Xeeon City Prison. "You are just one more criminal who needs to spend the rest of his days behind bars. Just wait patiently, because there are several J bots already on their way here, and once they arrive, justice will be served at last."

J997! Konoa says. *I thought you said no one would notice us.*

I thought no one would, but I guess I must have been mistaken. In my defense, I don't know every little part of the Brain. I know quite a bit, but my knowledge of it is hardly comprehensive. For security reasons, you understand.

Security reasons? Konoa repeats. *Why didn't you mention this before?*

I guess I didn't see my ignorance becoming a problem. I now see that I was wrong about that.

You're so—oh, never mind, Konoa says. *Look, let's just figure out how to get out of here before those other J bots arrive and arrest us.*

Well, I don't know what you expect me to do, seeing as I have very little power down here. I don't even have a body, aside from

133

your own, which I am currently unable to act independently of.

You're useless, you know that? Konoa snaps at me.

Only in this situation. If I had not offered you my knowledge of the Brain, we would not have even gotten this far.

It doesn't matter if this is as far as we can get if we can't get out of here, Konoa says. *Come up with something—*anything*—to get us out of here. I'm all ears.*

I consider the situation. Right now, the Brain has us pretty well captured. With its tentacles wrapped firmly around Konoa's arms, that severely restricts our movements. His legs dangle several feet above the floor, which also limits our options considerably. Not to mention that the J bots will be here any minute, which gives us even less time to think of an escape plan.

It is a very perplexing situation we have found ourselves in, one that is not made any easier by Konoa's frustrated attitude. Even though I am a machine, I find myself being affected by his attitude, probably because of our connection. This makes it harder to think, but think I must, because it is now up to me to come up with a way out of here.

Then an idea occurs to me, and I say to Konoa, Konoa, I have an idea.

What is it? Konoa asks. His mental voice sounds a little strained, most likely due to the stress that the Brain is putting on his body. *Speak quickly, because I don't know how much time we have to talk.*

I need to communicate with the Brain, which means you need to give me control over your vocal chords for a moment. I promise it won't be forever; just long enough for me to speak with it.

RETALIATION

What? Konoa says. *Give up control over my voice? Is that even possible?*

I believe it is. The Third Eye is connected to your frontal lobe. All I need to do is control that part and I will be able to make you say what I need you to say.

That doesn't sound very reassuring to me, Konoa says. *What are you going to say to the Brain?*

What I need to say to it. Anyway, will you let me speak through you? I have no time to explain it to you. It is faster if you just let me speak.

Fine, Konoa says. *But I am only doing this because I trust that you have come up with a way to get us out of here. If you are doing it for any other reason—*

I would think you would know if I had more malicious reasons for why I am doing this, considering how closely connected we are at the moment.

All right, Konoa says. *But be quick about it; remember, we don't have time for a long conversation.*

I will be so quick about it that you will think the Speedster himself spoke through you.

Speedster? Konoa repeats. *Isn't that a reference to that Xeeonite comic book character?*

It is. Well, technically, it's supposed to be a humorous reference, but—

Here? Really? Konoa interrupts, not bothering to hide the annoyance in his voice. *A joke? Come on. This is not the time or situation to share stupid jokes like that.*

I apologize. I was just trying to 'lighten the mood,' as Mad-Hammer Hagan says.

Just take control of my voice, Konoa says. *But if you try to make me say any of your stupid jokes, I* will *retake control even if that means messing up your plan. Understood?*

Yes, yes, I understand. No jokes. Besides, the Brain can't even comprehend humor, so telling it jokes would be a waste of time.

With that, I then take control of Konoa's vocal chords. It is not a difficult or complicated feat; all I do is transfer my thoughts through the Third Eye into his brain, which then sends a signal to the rest of his body to speak.

"Brain," I say aloud, speaking through Konoa's lips, which are not nearly as convenient for speaking through my own, but I master them quickly enough. "I am J997, a J bot law enforcer, speaking through this human's vocal chords."

"J997?" the Brain repeats. "Ah, yes. The Database said that you disappeared in Dela two and a half weeks ago, shortly after allegedly murdering almost a dozen Knights of Se-Dela. Your current whereabouts are listed as unknown."

"Well, now you can change that," I say. I slightly slur the words, because I am not used to speaking with an organic mouth and tongue. "Because I am right here, in front of you, albeit not in my original body."

"How are you speaking through that criminal, anyway?" the Brain asks. "Is there some kind of computer chip implanted in his brain that allows you to use his vocal chords to speak to me?"

"It does not matter how I am doing it," I say. It feels a little odd to hear Konoa's voice speaking aloud, rather than my own, but I keep talking anyway. "What matters is that you have apprehended a J bot law enforcer, who has committed no crimes whatsoever. Let the 'criminal'—which I can assure you that this human is not—go. Otherwise, I will report your insubordination to the Database once I regain my original body."

I look at the Brain's blinking red eye as I say that. Technically, of course, the Brain does not have any eyes or optics or anything else with which to see us, but it is easier to focus on one object and direct your words to it than it is to look aimlessly around and speak to nothing in particular.

"But the criminal entered without authorization from the Database or some other authority," the Brain says. "He made it past the security measures intended to keep me safe, likely with plans to sabotage my systems and free the prisoners I keep behind bars. I am only doing what I am supposed to do in a situation like this."

"You have still apprehended a J bot," I say. "Besides, how do you know this human's motivations? Have you suddenly gained telepathy? I doubt it. You are making assumptions not based on evidence or logic."

"Why should I listen to you?" says the Brain. "You have been missing for two and a half weeks without reporting back into the Database. That is in itself worthy of punishment. I should hand you over to the Database to be punished for your lack of communication with us regarding your whereabouts over the past two and a half weeks."

"By doing so, you will reveal that you arrested a J bot law enforcer," I point out. "That means you, too, will receive a punishment of some sort."

"You must think I am an organic being, scared of punishment, to think that will work on me," says the Brain. "If I must be punished for my 'crime,' then so be it. At least I will have ensured the complete safety of the prisoners housed within me, which is more than I can say for you."

Doesn't seem to be listening to us, J997, Konoa says. *Think we should try something else?*

I ignore Konoa's words. "I see that you are being stubborn and unreasonable for no reason."

"It is not for 'no reason,'" says the Brain. "It is *you* who have given me no reason to let the criminal go. He is clearly not a member of the maintenance crew, because he does not wear the maintenance crew's uniform, nor is there any information on him in the Database. In fact, he closely resembles a criminal who, earlier this morning, caused a panic in the streets by tossing a blind bomb into a crowd of innocents. That by itself is a crime that will earn you a one year prison sentence at least."

Looks like there's no fooling him, says Konoa. *If he knows that I'm the same guy who did that, then I think it's pretty clear we can kiss this plan good bye.*

I continue to ignore Konoa in order to focus on the Brain. "It is true that this man is the same human who tossed that blind bomb into that crowd of innocents, but did you know that he was hired to do so by Xacron-Ah?"

The Brain does not respond for a moment, as if it is trying to understand what I just said. "Xacron-Ah? The Mayor? That is impossible. Xacron-Ah went missing around the same time that this criminal threw the blind bomb into the crowd of innocents. Besides, if the Mayor was in contact with this criminal, I would know."

"Would you?" I say. "It isn't your job to know about the Mayor's every plan and movement and acquaintance. Your job is to keep prisoners within your walls. There is much you don't know about the Mayor and what he does. I wouldn't be so confident in your knowledge about him if I were you."

"That ... is true," says the Brain, with reluctance in its voice. "The Mayor doesn't tell me about everything he does. Still, why would the Mayor hire this criminal? The Mayor hates crime as much as us."

"Because this 'criminal,' as you call him, is part of a secret plan created by the Mayor to deal with crime in this city once and for all," I say. "Even I am a part of it. When I disappeared, it was because I had to work behind the scenes under the Mayor's secret but direct orders. I could not do what I had to do by working in the public eye, or even where my fellow J bots could see me."

"I have never heard of this 'plan,'" says the Brain in a skeptical voice. "Nor does the Database's files have anything on it. What does this 'plan' entail? How is it supposed to end crime in Xeeon once and for all?"

I sense Konoa listening just as much as the Brain, because he is as ignorant of this 'plan' as the Brain is. No surprise there; I did not even know of this plan myself until I made it up just now.

"It is a top secret plan, because if it were public and known in the Database, then every criminal in the world would know how to fight against it," I say. I hear Konoa's voice starting to strain slightly, likely due to the stress that the Brain is putting on his arms. "As for what the plan entails, that, too, is top secret, but I see that I must tell you about it now."

"Speak, then," says the Brain. "I see no harm in listening to your 'plan.' I will even record it so that I have evidence to hand over to the officers when they come to take you away. They can then verify whether this 'plan' you mention even exists."

I do not like the idea of the Brain recording our conversation; on the other hand, it is not like I am going to be revealing any actual information or knowledge that needs to be kept secret. The story I am about to tell is, after all, nothing more than an elaborate deception designed to make the Brain free us.

So I say, "All right, then. The plan is simple: the Mayor has disappeared in order to cause an illusion of insecurity in the city. He is hoping that this will draw out the more dangerous and difficult-to-capture criminals, who will undoubtedly use this time to commit even greater crimes than usual due to the fact that the J bots are searching for him. What the criminals don't realize, however, is that this will allow the J bots, following the Mayor's secret orders, to arrest them. This human's role in this plan is to cause more chaos in order to add to the realism of the deception, while my being framed for the murders of those Knights was supposed to convince the most dangerous criminals that we J bots were going rogue and therefore were far less likely to arrest them."

The Brain is silent for a few seconds, probably processing my plan. Then it says, "I see. That is a rather elaborate plan based on several factors that it seems to me that neither the Mayor nor the J bots control. I consider it an even riskier plan when you consider how a Lawful Ship has recently been dispatched to the Dead Lands in response to an anonymous tip about a group of criminals performing dangerous illegal activity out there, which has already split the J bots' numbers. No doubt this will make it even harder for them to arrest criminals, especially the dangerous ones you mention."

"I know it is difficult to believe, but this is what the Mayor thought was best and he explained it to me himself in similar words," I say. "If you decide to get in our way, you will only risk messing up the Mayor's plan to make the city a safer place for all."

"I still see no proof of this plan," says the Brain. It tightens its tentacles' grip around Konoa's arms, sending more pain signals into his brain, though I try to ignore them to focus on the situation at hand. "On the other hand, I am nothing more than a simple prison. It is not my job to judge the plans of the Mayor. And I doubt you are lying, J997, because you have a reputation of telling the truth, so perhaps you are being honest here as well."

I can feel Konoa's disbelief at the fact that my plan is working. Of course it is; I know how the Brain and J bots in general tend to think, so I understand the best ways to deceive us. We machines are not as good at detecting deception as we tend to think we are, at least when it comes from the mouths of our fellow J bots.

"Then why did you two sneak down here like a couple of common crooks, if you are working directly for the Mayor?" asks the Brain.

"The Mayor wanted us to find out if any arrests had been made since his disappearance," I say. "He is isolated from the rest of society at the moment, so he does not have access to the news. We know he has only been 'missing' for a few hours now, but crime moves fast, so the Mayor sent us down here to find out about any new arrests made this morning."

"Five arrests have been made since the Mayor's disappearance earlier this morning," says the Brain. "But there have yet to be any reports of an increase in criminal activity since the Mayor's

141

disappearance; that may be attributed to the fact that the J bots are keeping the Mayor's disappearance under wraps for the moment to avoid panicking the city's population, in addition to the fact that it only happened very recently."

"Then I will be sure to let the Mayor know once you let us go," I say. I nod at Konoa's arms. "So, if you will, could you please let us—"

An explosion of thunder interrupts my words, causing me to pull up Konoa's dangling legs without hesitation. As soon as I do, a hot, burning lightning bolt streaks underneath me, just barely missing the soles of Konoa's shoes, and strikes the red eye of the Brain.

The resulting explosion sends chunks of metal and glass flying toward us, but at the same time, the Brain's tentacles drop us to the floor. As soon as we land, we duck to avoid the worst of the shrapnel from the explosion, which is loud in our ears, but the explosion lasts less than a minute before its ends, allowing us to look up and see its results.

The Brain's mainframe is little more than fried circuitry now. Smoke rises from the twisted, blackened metal pit that was once its red eye, followed by the occasional spark from within. The tentacles from above hang limply, looking as dead as a corpse.

Meanwhile, the floor around us is covered in metal and glass and wires. Some of it got onto Konoa's body, but it is nothing serious or painful, although I do feel sharp pricks along his back and on his head.

Holy hell, says Konoa as we take our hands off our head. *What the hell was that?*

"Damn it," says a familiar, harsh and angry feminine voice

142

behind me. "Missed by *that* much."

We stand up and turn around to see who says that. Unfortunately, even I wish that we hadn't.

Standing in front of the entrance to the Brain is a tall, thin woman wearing witch's brown robes, her fingers glittering with ten skyras rings. Despite her youthfulness, her hair is stringy and gray, while her blackened and rotted teeth make me wonder how she is able to speak so fluently. Her skin is quite sickly and pale, but that does not make her look any less dangerous.

Raising her skyras rings before her, Jornan ah Kona says, "Well, I guess it doesn't matter that I missed you once. I have plenty of time to hit you again, even if you're a moving target. Just need to be a little bit more careful in my aim is all."

Chapter 6

Jornan ah Kona?" I say, staring at her in surprise. "How did you get here? How did you even know we were here?"

Jornan chuckles darkly. "I was here in the city overseeing a shipment of super speed from Dela when I got a call from the Founder. Told me that our Xeeonite base was under attack by a bunch of those stupid J bots and that he needed me to go to the Brain and stir up some shit here to distract them."

"What do you mean?" I say. "Are you saying that you came here to destroy the Brain?"

"Essentially, because with Xacron-Ah's kidnapping, we don't really need the Brain anymore," says Jornan, nodding. "But he also told me to go and kill any Foundation members operating in Xeeon, because he thought you guys were here. Looks like he was right. Old bastard."

She says that with some affection, like she thinks the Founder is not really an old bastard. Not that that makes her any less threatening, however.

"Anyway, I think I've seen ya before," says Jornan, gesturing at us. "You're Konoa, right? You and some of your friends destroyed one of our super speed gardens on Dela, if I'm not mistaken, about five years back, right?"

I feel Konoa retake control of his mouth. "Yeah, that was me.

144

And I would have killed you, too, if the Head had given me orders to."

"As if an ordinary human like you could ever do that," says Jornan, shaking her head. "I could kill you with my pinkie finger if I wanted. But I guess you can go ahead and think you're all that. No skin off my bones."

Konoa steps back, even though there is nowhere for us to run to. "I don't understand why you destroyed the Brain. Don't you realize that will cause the release of some of Xeeon's worst criminals?"

"What do I care?" says Jornan. "What does it matter? The Founder said this is supposed to be a distraction and that, with the Mission so close to completion, it doesn't matter whether a bunch of criminals are running around the city freely or not. Besides, quite a few of these criminals were my friends or accomplices, so if they manage to escape and avoid getting killed by those guards, they can rejoin my gang and make me more powerful than before."

"But one of those prisoners is one of our own," says Konoa. "Kojama. You remember him, right?"

Jornan shrugs. "And? He'll probably get killed in all of the confusion. Though now I know why you are down here; you were trying to rescue him. Ha! This is even better than what I hoped for."

She says that while her rings continue to glow ominously. I recall that she can shoot lightning, create illusions, use telepathy, and block telecommunications, but I do not know what her other six rings do. And I do not really want to find out the hard way, to be honest.

"You picked a lousy time to show up," says Konoa. He jerks his thumb over his shoulder at the destroyed Brain. "Because the Brain said that he summoned several J bots when he caught us. They were supposed to arrest us, but seeing as you are a wanted criminal, I bet they'll arrest you as well once they see you."

"Those bastards can try," says Jornan. "Of course, I'll just blow them into little pieces if they so much as lay a finger on me. I almost killed one of those dumb machines a couple of weeks ago, back on Dela. Wonder where that freak is now."

I know exactly who she is referring to: myself. Several Knights of Se-Dela and I were trying to bust her crime gang, but due to a series of unfortunate events, the other Knights were killed by her lizard humanoids and I barely escaped with my own life.

I take control of Konoa's voice and jerk his thumb at his chest. "Are you referring to me, Jornan? Because I am right here, you know."

Jornan blinks in confusion. "You're not a robot."

"Technically, you are correct," I say. "This is Konoa's body, but thanks to a special computer chip, I, J997, share it with him. Do you remember me now?"

"J997," Jornan repeats. A look of deep concentration comes over her face as she thinks about that. Then she snaps her fingers and says, "Oh, yeah. I remember now. You're that dumb robot that Palos rescued from me back on Dela, aren't ya?"

"The one and the same," I say. "I was supposed to arrest you back then, but I failed to do so due to circumstances outside of my control."

"So what are you going to do, try to bring me in again?" says

Jornan.

"No," I say, shaking my head. "But if you get in my way, I will defeat you and leave you here for my fellow J bots to arrest."

"You couldn't beat me with your original body, so what makes you think you can beat me as a stupid computer chip in a pitiful fleshly body?" Jornan asks with a laugh. "By the way, how is Palos? I haven't heard anything about her since she teleported you away from me."

"She is dead," I say. "Killed by one of your Elders in cold blood back on Dela."

"Really?" says Jornan, a gleeful smile crossing her lips. "That's great. She's been in my way for too long now. Did she die screaming and begging for mercy?"

"She died trying to stop your plans," I say. "And while Palos and I were not the closest of friends and did not know each other very long, I cannot ever see her begging for mercy from anyone."

"Whatever," says Jornan. "What matters now is that the Mission is almost complete, according to the Founder. Won't be long now before the worlds are healed, as the Founder always says."

Her yellow ring begins crackling with electricity. "Sadly, you two idiots are not going to live long enough to see the brand new world that will emerge from the ruins of the old worlds, nor will you get to see me become the queen of my own empire, as the Founder promised me."

She shoots a lightning bolt at us. We dive to the side, behind one of the servers, as the lightning bolt strikes the Brain's central computer again, causing another explosion that sends shrapnel flying everywhere. We roll to our feet behind the server before

147

moving again, just in time to avoid another lightning bolt that fries the server completely.

"Come out, come out, wherever you are!" Jornan calls out in a playful, but dangerous, voice. "'Cause I'm going to fry you so badly that even your mother won't be able to recognize your corpse!"

We stop behind another group of servers, but do not move. Instead, we keep as quiet as possible, even while listening to Jornan as she draws closer to the Brain's center.

Okay, J997, what's the plan? Konoa asks. *You've fought her before. What should we do?*

It should be noted, Konoa, that the last time I fought her, she almost successfully turned me into scrap. I only survived because Palos teleported me away. So I am afraid that I don't really have any 'plan' with which to deal with her, unfortunately.

Sure would be nice if we had Palos here, Konoa says. *But come on. You have to know* something *about her. Does the Database—*

I have no connection to the Database right now. I don't even have the mobile Database, because this compressed format cannot hold all of the mobile Database's files. I have my basic personality files, most of my memories, and all of the files on the Xeeon City Prison and the surrounding area. Nothing else besides that.

Nothing on Jornan, then? Konoa says.

Nothing. Besides, the Database has little information on her anyway. So even if I had complete and uninhibited access to the entire Database, that still would not be very helpful for us.

Damn it, Konoa says, slamming his fist against the server we are hiding behind. *Okay, so we need to come up with a plan. I wish I had some kind of weapon to fight back with.*

Our best chance at victory would be to disable Jornan's rings. We must either remove them from her fingers or break them.

But that requires getting up close to her, says Konoa. *And if we get close to her, she'll fry us.*

Well, I don't know what else to do, then. We just need to figure out a good way to get her rings without her killing us. There must be someway to do it.

We need to distract her somehow, Konoa says. *Only question is, how?*

Before I can answer that, Jornan shouts, "Come out and show yourself, you bastards!"

This is followed by a loud explosion that sends more wiring and glass and metal flying through the air over our heads. Konoa dashes away from our hiding place among the servers, making his way to another set of servers nearby. We hide within, again keeping quiet as we listen to Jornan stomping around the place and demanding that we show ourselves.

And then there's also the J bots that are coming, Konoa says. *Assuming they actually succeed in arresting Jornan, they'll also arrest us unless we can somehow miraculously escape. I just don't like this situation we're in. That's all.*

You need to be more confident, Konoa. There is always a way out of a situation, no matter how grim the odds. We know that destroying her rings is what we need to do. So we just need to figure out how to do it.

Like I said, we need a distraction so we can get up close to her without her killing us instantly, says Konoa. *I just don't know* how *we can distract her, though.*

I consider his idea, even as the sounds of Jornan tearing the place apart make Konoa's heart beat faster. We have very little time to think of a way to stop her, so I must think quickly before she finds and kills us.

We are in the Brain and—Ah ha!

Ah ha? Konoa repeats. *What does that mean?*

We need to reach one of the Brain's computers.

How? Konoa says. *Aren't they all too damaged to work? I mean, Jornan blew up the central computer. Doesn't that mean that the Brain is useless?*

Not unless we activate its backup generator. If we can do that, then that will reboot the Brain and allow it to take care of Jornan for us. It's our best option at the moment, because the Brain is equipped to deal with a variety of threats to its well-being, including Delanian witches that want to murder innocent people.

Guess it's better than nothing, Konoa says. *All right, how do we activate the backup generator?*

The manual switch should be on the back of the central computer. All Jornan has done is destroy the front; if we can get to the back and flip the manual switch on, it should not only activate the backup generator, but also activate the Brain's automatic defense systems.

Guess I'll have to make a run for it, then, Konoa says. *Here I go!*

Konoa stands up and dashes out from our hiding place. As soon as he does so, Jornan shouts, "There you are!" and teleports in front of us. She raises her crackling lightning bolt ring, her rotted teeth displayed in the wicked grin on her mouth.

150

"Thanks for showing yourself, ya dumb … well, whatever you are," says Jornan. "You saved me hours of—"

Konoa punches her in the face before she can finish her sentence. The blow sends her staggering, almost tripping over her feet. He then follows it up with a kick to her side, sending Jornan falling to the floor with a stunned look on her face.

We then run past her, heading for the back of the Brain's central computer as fast as Konoa's legs can run. He is in much better shape than I thought, because he does not slow down or become even slightly winded as we run.

Behind us, Jornan shouts, "Oh, no you don't! Get back here!" followed by the sound of thunder echoing loudly in the chamber.

Konoa and I drop to the floor as a lightning bolt sails over our heads. Looking up, we watch as the lightning bolt strikes a server, causing it to explode and send shrapnel into its neighbors. This causes the other servers to catch fire, which makes me wonder just how much all of this destruction is going to cost the city later.

Konoa is not curious about this, however. He rises to his feet and runs again, but as before, Jornan teleports in our path, scowling at us more angrily than ever.

"Idiots," says Jornan. "Where do you think you are running to? There's nowhere for you to go here. Why don't you save us some time and die already?"

Konoa tries to punch her again, but this time Jornan blocks the punch with her arm and grabs Konoa's neck with her other hand. Displaying more physical strength than I thought she had, she lifts Konoa off his feet and throws him to the right.

We hit the floor hard, the impact making Konoa gasp in pain. I urge him to get back up, however, because we have no time to lie here when Jornan is around.

Konoa manages to get back to his feet, grabbing a sharp piece of metal for a weapon as he does so, but before we can do anything, Jornan is in front of us again. All of her rings are crackling with energy now, making her look even more dangerous and psychotic than before.

She slaps Konoa across the face, sending him staggering backward from the blow. He shakes his head as Jornan advances on us, her eyes gleaming as dangerously as her rings.

"You Foundation agents were always weak," says Jornan as her black ring glows brighter than the others for a moment. "And now look at what we've reduced you to. Are you the only Foundation agent still alive or just the only survivor still loyal to the Head? Doesn't matter, because I am going to kill you like you deserve."

Konoa hesitates and looks around in confusion, despite the fact that Jornan is right there in front of us, still advancing with every intent to kill us.

Konoa, what are you doing? Jornan is still there. What are you looking for?

But I don't see her, says Konoa as he takes a step back. *Don't hear her or smell her or anything. It's like she vanished into thin air.*

Vanished into—? That makes no sense. I can still see her through your eyes.

You can? Konoa says. *But how?*

She must be using her rings to cast an illusion on you. She is making it seem like she has disappeared, when in fact she has not gone anywhere. It obviously does not affect me because I am a

152

machine and we cannot be affected by magic-induced illusions like organics can, so I can see through her illusions that fool you.

Oh, says Konoa. *But that still doesn't change the fact that I can't see her, which means I can't hit her.*

Wait until I tell you to strike and give me some control over the arm and hand in which you hold that chunk of metal. She's still coming closer and it won't be long before she is within your reach. But continue to pretend to be fooled by her illusion; we don't want her to suspect that her ring hasn't fooled us both.

If you say so, says Konoa, the uncertainty in his voice great.

I look at Jornan again. She is close now, her yellow ring still crackling with energy. She points her finger with the yellow ring on it at us, but she apparently wants to use it up close and personal, rather than fire it at a distance, because she is still walking toward us. I can even see the whites of her crazed eyes, but she is still not close enough yet for Konoa to attack.

"The Founder is going to be mighty pleased with me once he learns I killed you," says Jornan, even though she must know that Konoa cannot hear her. "It will be sweet, knowing I helped take out one more obstacle between us and completing the—"

Now, Konoa! Strike her throat!

Konoa does not say anything in response. He just lunges forward, with his piece of shrapnel held before him, and grabs Jornan's extended arm. Jornan lets out a shout of surprise before Konoa, with my guidance, stabs the metal piece directly into her throat.

Blood shoots out from Jornan's throat, some of it getting on Konoa's face, but most of it bleeds out onto Konoa's hand that is still shoving the metal piece into her throat. Jornan gasps for air and pushes us away, causing Konoa to let go of the sharp metal piece, but the damage is done. Even as we watch, Jornan collapses onto the floor, gasping and coughing up blood, weakly grabbing at the metal lodged in her throat, but she even stops doing that quickly enough. Soon, she is as still as a rock. Her neck continues to bleed, but Jornan herself appears quite dead, although without my normal body's sensors, that is impossible for me to confirm at the moment.

That ... was ... close, says Konoa, panting and wiping the sweat off his forehead with his other hand that does not have blood on it. *But it worked. I thought for sure she was going to kill us, but she didn't. Thanks for the help. Couldn't have done it without you.*

As I said, just because our situation looks grim does not mean that we are destined to fail. Through proper thinking and creativity, we successfully survived. Although I do wish we hadn't killed her, because I'd much rather have arrested her and brought her to justice to answer for her crimes.

What matters is that we are alive and she isn't, Konoa says. Then he starts. *Oh, crap. I almost forgot. The Brain's J bots are still coming. We have to get out here before they find us.*

I agree. But what about Kojama?

There's nothing we can do about Kojama right now, says Konoa. *We'll have to come back for him at a later time. Unless you want to spend the night with him in prison, that is.*

No, I don't.

Then you understand why we have to leave right away, even if that makes this mission into a failure, says Konoa. He turns around toward the exit *If we leave now, we might be able to get back to headquarters before the J bots that the Brain summoned arrive.*

All right. But before we go, grab Jornan's skyras rings.

Konoa stops with one foot in the air. *Why?*

Because we might be able to make good use of them. Plus, I have always wanted to know the full extent of her powers to document in the Database, so I believe that this is a great opportunity to accomplish that task.

Good point, Konoa says. *I don't want Reunification somehow getting their hands on her rings and giving them to another one of their agents anyway.*

So Konoa turns back around, removes all ten skyras rings from Jornan's fingers as quickly as he can, and stuffs them into his pockets. Konoa then stands up and makes a break for the exit.

Even as we do so, loud alarms blare all around us, but we pay little attention to that because we are too focused on escaping to care.

Chapter 7

We successfully escape from the Brain and climb out of the sewers into the alleyway we had been in before. One look in the direction of the Xeeon City Prison itself shows that the gates have opened on their own and the guards are flying and running along the walls and perimeter of the Prison, shouting orders to the prisoners and advice to each other. I even see one prisoner wrestling with one of the guards before another J bot comes up behind the prisoner and shoots him in the back of the head, causing the prisoner to fall off the wall and land with a *thud* on the street below, the impact breaking the back of his head open and causing blood and brains to flow out.

Not only that, but loud alarms are going off all at once, so loud that they are almost deafening. That is not even counting the sounds of paralyzing repulser blasters—also known as PRBs— being shot and prisoners and guards alike screaming incoherently. I see the lights turn on in the windows of some of the nearby buildings and even a few Xeeonian citizens sticking their heads out the windows in confusion (a handful appear to be yelling back, although what they are yelling, I have no idea).

Three prisoners sprint from the gates, but before they can get far, about a dozen guards swoop in from above and fire just as many PRBs at them. The prisoners collapse under the firepower, although whether they are dead or simply unconscious, I cannot tell from our current position.

The situation is way more chaotic than I thought, Konoa says. *I mean, look at how all of the J bots are flying around trying to restore order and keep the prisoners from escaping. The destruction of the Brain must have completely messed with their security systems.*

Of course it did. The Brain is what controlled the entire Prison, even to a certain extent influencing the behaviors and thoughts of the guards. Now that it is destroyed, it comes as no shock to me that utter confusion and chaos have resulted. I imagine that the guards will restore a sense of order soon enough, however, because these guards are that efficient. In the meantime, we should return to headquarters and report back to the Head on the success of our mission.

Konoa, however, lingers in the alley, looking at the chaotic scene playing out around and inside the prison. In particular, he is looking at the open gates.

Konoa? What are you thinking?

Well, I thought that we wouldn't have any time to save Kojama after we killed Jornan, says Konoa. *But now ... well, just look at this chaos. If we're smart, we might be able to go in and save him. The guards might not even notice us entering or getting away in the confusion.*

That seems like an unwise move to me. The guards of the Xeeon City Prison are not afraid to kill anyone who is not supposed to be here and who is acting illegally. Or they may mistake you for a prisoner and still try to kill you; in any case, we would do better to return to headquarters and make another plan there.

Are you kidding me? Konoa asks. He gestures at the chaotic prison. *Just look at all of this chaos and confusion. If we don't take advantage of it now, the J bots will restore order and then begin Kojama's execution. We don't have time to return home and make a new plan. We have to do it now, while the time is right.*

The time does not seem right to me, Konoa. There is an extremely high chance that the guards will capture or kill us if we go in there now.

Konoa immediately jams his fingers into his pockets and pulls out Jornan's skyras rings. *Then I'll use these to protect us. I'm not much of a wizard, but I understand the general principle behind skyras rings well enough to know how to use them in a basic way. Besides, I doubt these guards expect me to use magic, so that's another advantage we have over them.*

But we don't even know what half of them do. You could end up hurting us if you use them.

But if we don't do *anything, then Kojama* will *die,* Konoa argues. *Anyway, why do I need your approval? This is my body. If I say we are going to take advantage of this confusion and rescue Kojama, then that's what we're going to do. Plain and simple.*

It isn't that plain or that simple, Konoa, and you know it.

Unfortunately, Konoa stops listening to me. He dashes toward the prison, slipping Jornan's skyras rings onto his fingers as he does so, doubled over as low as he can to avoid attracting attention or being hit by the lasers shooting all over the place.

Konoa soon reaches the walls, which he runs along as close as he can to avoid being spotted by the J bots. It is a bit useless, seeing as the city and prison lights are shining all around us, but in the confusion and chaos surrounding the Prison, we have still not been spotted by anyone.

When we reach the gates, one of the guards flies down in front of us, blocking our path. It raises its PRB and aims it toward us, saying, "Halt. You are under arrest for attempting to trespass on —"

The guard does not get an opportunity to finish its sentence, because Konoa points his index finger—the one with Jornan's yellow lightning bolt ring—at the guard. A lightning bolt lances out and strikes the guard in the head, instantly making it explode. Konoa then dashes through the gates as the guard's headless body falls to the ground.

We emerge into the courtyard of the Prison, which is full of prisoners and guards alike fighting each other. One of the guards slams the butt of its PRB in the face of one of the prisoners and then kicks him in the stomach, sending the prisoner falling to the ground. On the other side of the courtyard, a dozen human prisoners are fighting against three guards, though the fight seems to be tilting in the guards' favor based on how their PRBs are hitting the human prisoners in vital spots.

I want to help the guards capture the prisoners and return them to their cells, but I am powerless to do so because Konoa has complete control over his body at the moment. I try to tell him that I want to help—it is in my programming, after all—but he ignores me as he scans the courtyard for a path to take us into the Prison itself. That is difficult, because the courtyard is so full of battling guards and prisoners that it more closely resembles a battlefield than a Prison.

But then Konoa pulls out one of Jornan's rings—the gray

teleportation ring—and activates it. The world around us becomes dark for a moment before we appear right back into the lights and noise of the prison courtyard; only this time, we are on the other end of the courtyard, near the entrance to the Prison itself, where the sliding doors appear to have been smashed open by the prisoners themselves in an attempt to get free.

We then dash inside the Prison, and as soon as we do, the sounds of battle outside become muted. We are now in the Prison lobby, where a clear glass wall that once divided the rest of the prison from the lobby is shattered and where a couple of fallen J bots lie, apparently having been trampled by the escapees based on their flattened and crushed bodies.

All right, J997, says Konoa, looking around the Prison's lobby. *Which way should I go?*

I am not sure. I do not know what cell Kojama is being kept in. I have not had a chance to reconnect with the Database, so I have not been able to update my files on the prisoners held within this place. For all we know, Kojama might have escaped in the confusion already, which means that us going in here to rescue him is as fruitless as I thought.

Seems unlikely to me, says Konoa. *While Kojama is by no means the kind of guy to just sit back and let everyone else rescue him, I think the Head would have contacted us by now if Kojama had escaped on his own. He's probably still in here somewhere.*

Maybe you are right. But if he's not, then we are severely risking our safety and our freedom by going in here. Even if most of the guards are outside trying to keep the rest of the prisoners from escaping, it won't be long before some of them return here, at which point we will be caught.

160

RETALIATION

Not unless we are fast, says Konoa. *Now, J997, do you know where prisoners on death row are usually kept? Do they have a special holding cell in here for those prisoners?*

Yes, they do. It is located in the east wing, near the execution chamber, where most executions are typically carried out. Sometimes they don't take prisoners there, so Kojama might not be there at all, but that is our best bet.

Gee, I would never have figured out on my own that the execution chamber is where most executions happen, says Konoa. *So east wing, was it?*

Yes, but again, this is dangerous and I do not suggest that you go there, even with all of the prison's security systems off. It's too risky. We could be caught.

What did I say about this being my *body?* Konoa says as he runs across the shattered glass covering the floor and past the smashed reception desk. *Just give me the directions, since you have the map and all.*

As much as I still disagree with our current course of action, I decide that I can at least help Konoa find Kojama so that we can decrease the likelihood of us being caught. So I tell Konoa when to turn, what routes to take, and any shortcuts I see on the map of the prison's interior, even as I continue to think that this is sheer, short-sighted foolishness on his part. I am not the kind of robot to look down on humans for their flaws, but I am now starting to understand why some of my fellow machines do.

We run past multiple open prison cells, each one empty, though they will be full again soon enough if the guards here do their job. Konoa just glances at them long enough to ascertain that Kojama is not still inside them before turning his attention to the next cell.

The sounds of battle are much more muted now. Due to the thick walls of the prison, we cannot hear the battle between the guards and the prisoners anymore, which makes it impossible for us to know how the battle is progressing. Part of me still wants to go back and help my fellow J bots apprehend and return each escapee to his cell, but Konoa's will remains stronger than mine, so I can do nothing but continue to give Konoa directions as we enter the east wing of the prison.

Okay, J997, says Konoa as he glances up at a sign above the hallway that reads 'EAST WING' as we pass. *We're in the east wing now. Where would Kojama be kept, exactly?*

At the end of the hallway, there is a special cell reserved for death row inmates. Assuming he hasn't escaped yet, he should be in there awaiting his execution.

Konoa smiles. *Great. With Jornan's rings, we should be in and out before even Kojama realizes what's happening. Can't wait. He's going to be so happy to see us.*

The east wing's hall is longer than the other halls of the Prison, but that doesn't discourage Konoa, who runs down it anyway, although not as quickly as usual due to his tiredness. Still, he puts all of his extra strength into running as fast as he can, which surprises me, as I didn't think that Konoa and Kojama were that close.

Why would you think that? Konoa asks.

Because Lanresia told me that you are jealous of her and Kojama's closeness. I thought you might not be entirely enthusiastic about saving him, but you seem absolutely giddy now.

RETALIATION

I used to be jealous, until Lanresia and I sat down and had a good long talk about her exact relationship with him, says Konoa as we run. *Then I spoke with Kojama and got any misunderstandings out of the way. We became great friends after that, even though he always outclassed me in every way and we rarely went on missions together.*

Interesting. Lanresia made it sound like you are still jealous of him.

You know how women are, says Konoa, rolling his eyes. *Lanresia, in particular, seems to think that having two men fighting over her is desirable. I love her to death, but it can be pretty annoying how she puts her own spin on things that isn't always correct.*

I am afraid I do not understand why a woman would like it if two men are fighting over her.

You and me both, says Konoa. *Anyway, how much farther is that cell for death row inmates?*

Not much farther now, according to the map. Just keep running and we should get there in no time at all. In fact, I think we can see the door now; it's that open metal door at the end of the hall. Do you see it?

Konoa's smile grows even wider when he spots the door I am referring to. *Awesome. Once we get Kojama back, Reunification won't stand a chance.*

In a few seconds, we reach the special cell for death row inmates. Because the door is open, Konoa wastes no time in dashing inside, saying, "Kojama! It's me, Konoa! I am here to get you out of—"

He stops speaking quite abruptly when we see the scene we have stumbled upon. I at first am not sure why, but soon my compressed AI catches up with Konoa's brain and even I am shocked by what we see.

Kneeling on the floor, with his hands tied behind his back, is a human with pointed, elvish ears and two mechanical legs that look quite advanced. He has a mop of black hair that goes down to his shoulders, and he is wearing the standard prison uniform— gray and white—that all prisoners wear. His face is blooded and bruised, which appears to be the work of the guards based on the shape of the hand prints on his cheeks. He is even missing a few teeth, which makes him look even worse.

But it is not Kojama who we are looking at. No, our focus is on the woman standing before him, holding a PRB point blank to his forehead. Kojama's eyes dart in our direction, but he does not so much as utter one word when he sees us, nor does he move his head. He looks back up at the bald female elf who is holding the barrel of the gun to his head, a pleading, terrified look in his brown eyes.

Konoa tries to speak, but is unable to at first, until he finds his tongue and says, in a confused and horrified voice, "Lanresia … what are *you* doing here?"

Lanresia, the female elf who is holding the gun to Kojama's head, looks at us. She appears surprised that we are here, as if she did not expect to see us in this place. Her black concealment ring is glowing on her trigger finger, but it is not active at the moment.

"Oh, Konoa, J997," says Lanresia. Her gun hand is quite steady. "I didn't expect either of you to try to break into the Prison tonight. I thought you were going to abandon the mission and return to headquarters, what with the confusion and chaos caused by the Brain's failure making it difficult to break into here."

Konoa rubs his eyes and looks at her again. "But I thought ... why are you here? The Head said this was supposed to be our mission and our mission alone. I don't recall her telling you to help us."

"That's because you have it the other way around," says Lanresia. She nods at Kojama. "*You* are helping *me* kill Kojama. Rescuing him was never actually part of the plan."

"What the hell?" says Konoa. "You're wrong. The Head—"

"Only told you that because she knew you wouldn't be able to perform for the actual mission," Lanresia finishes for him. "Even though it is necessary if the Foundation is going to survive."

"Necessary?" says Konoa. "How is killing Kojama, our best agent, necessary for the Foundation to survive? This makes no sense."

"Because Kojama was kidnapped," says Lanresia, a hint of regret in her voice. She presses the tip of her gun deeper into Kojama's forehead. "I am supposed to kill him before he can reveal any secrets about the Foundation to our enemies. That was why the Head sent you two; by having you stir up chaos—which you did a really good job at, by the way—I could then slip in among the confusion, off Kojama here, and then slip out without anyone being the wiser."

"And then you would blame it on the guards or one of Kojama's fellow inmates once the news got out that Kojama was dead," says Konoa, understanding slowly rising in his voice. "Oh my god. It all makes sense now."

"You were never supposed to be here," says Lanresia. "You were supposed to return to headquarters, defeated, and then learn later on that poor Kojama was tragically killed in an escape attempt. I should have known you would try to save him anyway, however, because that's the man I fell in love with when I first joined the Foundation all those years ago."

She doesn't sound fearful or angry at all; merely disappointed. Somehow, that is much worse than if she was angry; at least, that is what Konoa is feeling about this. I myself am simply glad that my distrust of the Foundation was indeed based in fact.

"But you don't *have* to kill Kojama, you know," says Konoa, gesturing at his friend. "If all of us work together, we can get him out of here and maybe even rebuild the Foundation together."

Lanresia shakes her head. "You don't understand. You want to know why the Foundation is basically on life support? It is because of Kojama. He sold us out to Reunification. The traitor."

Tears appear in Lanresia's eyes when she says that, but she just wipes them away.

"Traitor?" says Konoa. "How is Kojama a traitor? I thought —"

"When he was captured after the assault on our Xeeonite branch, he promised to give Reunification vital information on how to find the Delanian branch," says Lanresia. "Not only that, but he gave them information on our Delanian base's systems and defenses so they could get past them, which is how they managed to crush us there, too. Isn't that right, Kojama?"

She says his name with disgust. Her finger does not yet pull down on the gun's trigger, but it is only a matter of time before it does so. I can even tell that the PRB has been set from stun to kill, as all PRBs have those two settings for the different purposes that we J bots use them for.

"How could you have found out about any of this, though?"

says Konoa. "We haven't had any contact with Kojama at all since he disappeared after the assault on the Xeeonite base. Maybe Reunification found out about the Delanian branch from some other way."

"The Head put it together," says Lanresia. "You know how much smarter she is than the rest of us. She looked at the evidence, put two and two together, and understood that Kojama is the reason behind our destruction. He is the reason Reunification is so close to accomplishing their Mission, which will bring about mass death unlike anything seen since the Separation; therefore, he must die."

Tears are streaming down Kojama's face as well. He has not spoke one word since we saw him, but there is no need, because even I can read the terror on his face. He clearly wants to be spared, but it seems unlikely to me that Lanresia will listen to any sort of reason in her current state of mind.

Konoa looks at Kojama and asks, "Brother, is any of what Lanresia just said true?"

Kojama still does not speak, but there is no denial in his eyes; only shame and fear.

"See?" says Lanresia, poking Kojama in the head with the gun's tip. "He betrayed us. All because he's a coward. We thought he was the best, the bravest, the kindest, and the greatest, but he's nothing more than a dirty traitor, a damn *pig*."

"But does that mean we must murder him in cold blood?" says Konoa. He holds out a hand toward Lanresia. "Lan, do you really think Kojama deserves death? I thought that that is what Reunification does to its traitors. Aren't we supposed to be better than they?"

"We are," says Lanresia, "which is why I want to kill this bastard. I don't care if this counts as murder; besides, it was the Head who gave me these orders. Who am I to go against the orders of the Head?"

"The Head ..." Konoa appears to have a hard time saying these next words. "The Head is not always right. Even if Kojama is a traitor, why must we kill him ourselves? He was supposed to be executed anyway, right? Why not let the executioner do his job? Why go through all of this trouble of trying to kill him when he was just going to be executed anyway?"

Lanresia gun hand still does not waver. She smirks at Kojama. "Did you hear that, Kojama? Your selling us out accomplished *nothing* either way. Even if I never came to kill you, the prison's executioner would have anyway. Betraying us really worked out well for you in the end, now didn't it?"

Kojama still says nothing. He appears too afraid to speak, probably because he believes that saying anything will hasten his death.

"But to answer your questions, Konoa," says Lanresia, looking at him again, "we are going to kill him because Kojama is a smart man who likely would have found a way out of here all on his own anyway. Then he would be free to go where he wants, to hide from us ... and there is no way the Head would tolerate such traitorous, cowardly behavior. Never. So as you can see, we were forced to kill him. It is our only option."

"But what is the point?" says Konoa. "The Foundation is already a shadow of what it used to be. It's not like Kojama telling others about our secrets will—"

"The Foundation is not dead," says Lanresia sharply. "We can still rebuild, but not if everyone and their Grand Lizard knows about us and our secrets. To ensure the continuation of the organization, we need to eliminate those who would put our revival at risk."

Kojama's tears are flowing freely now, but he is still not saying anything. I almost wonder if he is mute; then again, he is probably too afraid to speak in case he says something that will end in his head being blown off his shoulders.

"You sound just like an agent of Reunification," says Konoa. His words are harsher now; they have lost the gentleness he usually uses when speaking to Lanresia. "Always going on about the 'Mission,' about how you must kill anyone who poses even the vaguest threat to your organization. This is not what I signed up for."

"Too bad," says Lanresia, her speaking snake staring at us with as much intensity as her organic eyes. "The Head said that this is what we must do. And with Reunification's end coming any day now, that means that the time is ripe for us to rebuild in the shadows."

"But if Reunification falls, what is the point of the Foundation?" asks Konoa. "I thought that was the whole point of our organization: To stand against Reunification's efforts to reunite the worlds. Without Reunification, what purpose does the Foundation serve?"

Lanresia shrugs. "I don't know what else the Head has in store for us, but I do know that she wants to rebuild the Foundation stronger than ever. And in order to become strong, we must first eliminate the weak."

She nods at Kojama. "All I need to do is shoot him once—just once—and he will be dead. And there is nothing you can do to stop me."

Konoa grits his teeth, but even I can tell that there is nothing we can do to save Kojama. Under any other situation, we could have saved him; but now, if we try anything, she will simply kill Kojama, and possibly us as well.

"Anyway, I don't have a whole lot of time to talk with you," says Lanresia, shaking her head. "It won't be long before the guards restore order among the prisoners. Then they will come here to ensure that Kojama has not escaped and find us, which I cannot allow."

She begins to pull down on the trigger, prompting Konoa to shout, "Wait! Please don't do it, Lanresia. If you do—"

"What, will you harm me?" says Lanresia, looking at us in annoyance. "Of course you won't. You love me. I know you do. Even if you think I'm dead wrong, you still wouldn't hurt me, even if it hurting me meant saving the two worlds."

Konoa lowers his hand. "You're right. I wouldn't hurt you. I can't. Not when I love you more than my own life. But I know that you love me just as much as I love you, despite how harshly you've spoken to me."

Konoa raises his index finger—the one with Jornan's yellow skyras ring on it—and places it against the side of his head. Even I can feel the heat that the ring is generating, heat that gives me a glimpse of the power within the ring.

"What are you doing?" says Lanresia. She no longer sounds as confident as she did before; now, she sounds worried. "Why are you pointing your finger at your head like that?"

"One shot is all I need to end my life and J997's life as well," says Konoa. "This is Jornan ah Kona's lightning bolt skyras ring. If I fire it, I'll be dead instantly."

"That's a bad joke, Konoa, and you know it," says Lanresia. For the first time, I notice her gun hand shake. "Maybe J997's lack of a sense of humor is starting to get to you."

"This is all me, Lan," says Konoa. "J997 doesn't have as much influence over me as you think. One blast and I'll end myself and him with me."

Lanresia's organic face begins to sweat, while her speaking snake says, "Stop telling such bad jokes. You wouldn't do such a thing."

"I will," says Konoa. "Unless you agree not to kill Kojama, that is. Then I will not take my own life."

"This is unfair," says Lanresia. Her gun hand is even more unsteady now, but it is still too risky for Konoa to lower his finger from his head. "You're going to kill yourself, just to save a guy who you were jealous of when you first met him?"

"I don't consider it fair to ruthlessly murder anyone who betrays us, especially someone who I consider a friend," says Konoa. "Now you know the terms I've laid out for you. Either drop the gun and spare Kojama's life or I kill myself and J997."

Hold it, Konoa. I am not so sure—

Shut up, Konoa says. *I have a plan, don't worry. Lanresia loves me too much to let me do this.*

I still do not like putting my life into your hands like this.

But Konoa continues to ignore me. His eyes are locked on Lanresia's; not on her speaking snake's optics, but on her actual, organic eyes. He is daring her to follow the Head's orders. Yet even I cannot tell what Lanresia will do next.

171

Then Lanresia sighs and lowers her gun. "All right. You win, Konoa. I want to obey the orders I received from the Head, but I love you more than I love the Head, so I won't take Kojama's life."

Konoa smiles and lowers his index finger from his temple. "I knew I could count on you, Lan—"

Without warning, Lanresia raises her PRB and shoots it at us. The laser strikes Konoa in the chest, causing him to fall flat on his back on the floor. He tries to move, but the PRB's stunning laser locks his limbs in place, although he is able to raise his head in time to see Lanresia shoot Kojama in the head. Kojama falls to the floor, blood leaking from the burning hole in his forehead, as Lanresia walks up to us.

"Lanresia?" says Konoa, his words hard to speak, because of the PRB numbing his tongue. "What … why …"

"I am sorry, Konoa," says Lanresia. "But I had to do it. Don't worry, though; I won't kill you. I still love you. I'll just leave you here, where the guards can find you and lock you up. I'll tell the Head that you were captured and that I was unable to save you, but first …"

Lanresia lashes out with a powerful kick to Konoa's jaw. She must be stronger than she looks, because the blow breaks Konoa's jaw. I only know this because of the immense pain within it, which I can feel with Konoa, despite the numbing power of the PRB.

"There," said Lanresia. "Now you won't get a chance to tell the guards about the Foundation, while J997's compressed form doesn't have enough memories to pose a threat to our operations even if the Third Eye is surgically removed from your head and placed inside another computer—though the guards might just kill you anyway."

With that, Lanresia walks past us, even as Konoa struggles to undo the paralyzing effects of the PRB. But sheer willpower is not enough to overcome the laser's effects, especially with the pain from his broken jaw making it impossible for him to think straight.

Konoa tries to call Lanresia back, but his broken jaw makes speech impossible.

And now it is only a matter of time before the guards return and find us. And there is nothing we can do to escape before they do.

Excerpt:
Two Worlds Book #5:
Desinence

Chapter I

The little girl known as Kara ran through the tall grass with glee. She had no real destination in mind, except to run and run as quickly as she could. Today, after all, was the Day of Celebration, and her parents had said that she could have the whole day off from her boring as paint studies.

Her plan for the rest of the afternoon was simple. She would run around in the fields around their tiny little cottage for a few hours, return home for lunch, maybe play with her older brother and her Protector if they were around, and then go with her father to the Capital City in time for the celebration itself. Father had promised to buy her whatever gifts she wanted while they were in the City, partly due to the Day, but also partly due to how hard she had worked at her studies over the last year. She fully intended on asking Father for one of those neat, skyras-powered toy jet trains that her friend, Jana, had; they were so amazing, because they resembled real jet trains down to the last detail.

If I had that, I would be the most popular girl in town, Kara thought with a smile on her small lips.

But then, without warning, her small feet tripped over

1

something long and thick and she fell face first into the grass. She didn't break her nose or scratch her face; however, the fall did hurt, even when she put out her arms to break it.

Yet Kara was not a crybaby, like her brother always accused her of, so she didn't make even one sound when she fell. Instead, she turned around to see what she had tripped over, thinking maybe it was a stick she could play with, but she would have been forgiven if she had screamed her head off when she saw what it was, exactly.

The thing she had tripped over was a long, deadly-looking snake with green skin the same shade as the grass. Spikes rose up from its back like the back spikes of a dragon, and its raised its large, flat head to look at her with deadly red eyes. A low, deadly-sounding hiss emitted from its mouth, while the snake itself smelled like mud and dirt.

Kara had no interest in snakes or reptiles, which was why she was unable to identify this creature's species; however, she didn't need to be an expert on reptiles to know that this snake could swallow her whole if it wanted to. And considering how angry it looked, she had no doubt that it was planning to do that even as she watched it.

She scrambled to her feet and tried to walk backwards while keeping an eye on it, but she was never good at multitasking and so ended up almost falling over again. When Kara regained her balance, she just stood there in fear, staring at the snake's hypnotic red eyes as it drew closer to her.

Kara desperately wanted to cry out for her father, who she knew could kill this thing with his magic in one hit; but unfortunately, she was too paralyzed by fear to so much as whisper for help. She could only watch the monster snake draw closer and closer, its mouth opening wider and wider, revealing its fangs that looked sharper than any knife Kara had seen.

But at that moment, Kara heard someone running through the grass toward them. She did not know who it was, and neither did the snake, apparently, because it began looking around for the source of those running footsteps, which were getting closer and closer every second.

And then, without warning, a short, metal humanoid robot jumped out of the tall grass and tackled the snake to the ground. The snake hissed in anger and shock, while Kara gasped before she felt a familiar strong hand grab hers and a voice behind her say, "Come on, Kara! Let's get out of here!"

Kara looked over her shoulder and saw a boy of about ten pulling her through the tall grass. He had strawberry blonde hair and, when he glanced at her briefly, saw those natural blue eyes that she would recognize anywhere.

"Carem?" said Kara as her older brother pulled her along through the grass. "What are—"

"Vyll said he sensed you were in danger," Carem said without looking back at her. "I said he was just worrying too much about you, as usual, but he insisted we come out here and check on you anyway. Looks like he was spot on."

"That was Vyll back there?" said Kara, looking back in the direction they had came from, where she heard Vyll wrestling with the snake. "I've never seen him do *that* before."

"Well, he's supposed to be your Protector, isn't he?" said Carem. "That's what he's supposed to do, after all."

"Oh, I hope he's all right," said Kara, still glancing over her shoulder frequently. "That snake looked awfully mean."

"He'll be all right," said Carem. "He's strong. Protectors are tough."

"I hope you're right," said Kara. She felt the pockets of her dress and was relieved to feel that her picture was still folded up in there. "Because I have something special I want to share with him, something I've been meaning to give to him for a while. And I can't give it to him if the snake—"

A loud roar—with a vaguely snake-like hiss tingeing it—caused both Kara and Carem to stop in their tracks. They turned to look in the direction that the roar had come from, but they saw nothing except for the tall grass of the fields and the purplish hue of the sky above. And in the distance, the Seven Towers of Peace, but Kara could care less about the Seven Towers, because she now wondered if that roar had come from the snake, and if so, whether it was a roar of pain or a roar of victory. The roar abruptly cut off, but that did not make Kara feel any better about the fate of Vyll. She imagined the snake devouring Vyll whole, which made her stomach twist.

She and Carem watched as something made its way through the grass. It was hard to tell at first just who or what it was—indeed, for a moment, Kara almost thought that it might be the snake, having won its battle with Vyll—but soon she saw a familiar shine off a metallic head and her stomach untwisted.

"Vyll!" said Kara, waving at him as the Protector pushed his way through the grass. "Over here, boy!"

Her calling him must have encouraged him to come faster, because in seconds Vyll was right in front of Kara and Carem. He straightened up and saluted Kara both in that funny way he

4

Timothy L. Cerepaka

always did whenever he was reporting something to her.

"I have terminated the threat, Miss Kara," said Vyll. He gestured over his shoulder in the direction he had came. "The snake is dead. It won't be a threat to you or to brother Carem anymore."

Concerned over his well-being, Kara carefully observed Vyll's appearance. He was the same height as her and even had a similarly-shaped mouth like hers; aside from that, however, he looked completely different from her, as Protectors usually did. He had red eyes, for one (*Optics,* Kara corrected herself), and metallic skin that reflected the light of the twin suns in a pretty way. There was a weird green liquid covering his hands, but Kara knew that couldn't belong to him because Protectors like Vyll did not have blood. It was probably the blood of that snake, but she was so relieved at his survival that she didn't mind the blood on his hands.

Kara clapped her hands together excitedly. "That's great, Vyll! I was worried that you might get hurt. It was a big, mean old snake, after all, and it had really sharp teeth."

"My systems do not detect any injuries on my body," said Vyll. "Everything is functional, although I will need to oil my knee joints soon, because they are beginning to lose their nimbleness. I will also need to wash my hands of this blood."

"We can oil you when we get back to the house," said Kara. She looked up at her older brother. "Carem knows how to oil you. Right, Carem?"

"Sure do," said Carem, puffing his chest out. "Father showed me how to do it. I can do it in no time."

"Thank you for your offer, Miss Kara, Master Carem, but I do

5

not want to inconvenience you with my maintenance," said Vyll, as humbly as always. "Your mother is preparing lunch for you, after all, and by the time we get back, she will no doubt tell you to clean up and get ready to eat and then head to the City for the celebration. I doubt she will appreciate you getting your hands oily, which will make them very hard to clean even with soap and water."

Kara put her hands behind her back. "Yeah, I guess you're right, Vyll. Mother wouldn't be happy about that. Still, I want to give you *something* in return for your help. It's only fair."

"No need, Miss Kara," said Vyll. He jerked his thumb at his chest. "I am your Protector, after all, and have been since your birth. It is my duty to protect and guide you, even as I learn with you. The only reward I need is to see that you are safe and secure from all harm."

Carem sighed and looked back in the direction of the house with a wistful glance. "Wish I had a Protector. Too bad Father didn't let me get one 'cause I'm the oldest."

"I can be your Protector as well, Master Carem," said Vyll, holding out his hand to Carem. "Not officially, of course, but—"

"Eh, forget about it," said Carem, waving off Vyll's offer. "I'm strong on my own. First born always are. That's why we don't get our own Protectors."

Kara immediately knew that Carem was lying, because she heard the jealousy in his voice. Besides, while Carem was not a weak boy by any means, he was still far more brainy than brawn; he wasn't as strong as he thought he was (although he was taking sword fighting lessons from Master Hoyan, a retired Minister of Fariah who lived just down the road from their house).

She thought about teasing Carem for his pretending not to be jealous, but then she remembered the folded up picture in her pocket and snapped her fingers. "Oh! Vyll, I have something for you."

"Something for me?" said Vyll, who, Kara was pleased to see, did not seem to guess what she was going to show him. "What is it?"

"A gift," said Kara as she reached into the pockets of her dress and grabbed the picture.

"A gift?" said Vyll. He tilted his head to the side in that way Kara always thought made him look funny. "No one has ever given me a gift before. Not even on my birthday, which is tomorrow."

"*Our* birthday, you mean," said Kara. She pulled the folded-up picture from her dress and held it out for him. "Because we were both born on the same day, remember? Anyway, that's why I drew this picture for you. I knew that no one else was going to give you a present, so I decided to make sure you got at least one; after all, you don't turn nine every year."

Vyll looked at the folded-up picture for a moment before taking it. He got some of the still-fresh green blood on it, but he wiped the picture on the grass to clean it, although Kara didn't really care, because it was his present and he was allowed to do what he wanted with it.

"Unfold it," said Kara. "Come on. Don't you want to see what it looks like?"

Vyll unfolded the picture carefully, making sure not to rip or damage it. When he finished unfolding it, he looked at it like he wasn't even sure how to react to the drawing on it.

"So?" said Kara. "Do you like it? I drew it myself."

"Hey, I helped, too," said Carem, holding up one hand. "Went and bought the art supplies myself. So it was a team effort."

Vyll looked up from the picture. His expression was hard to read, but Kara thought he looked astonished.

"I … like it," said Vyll. He looked down at the picture again. He then began pointing at the figures that Kara had drawn on it. "That's me. And there's you, Miss Kara, and you as well, Master Carem. All three of us together."

"Of course we're together," said Kara with a smile. "I wanted to draw pictures of Mother and Father as well, but they're harder to draw, so I just went with us three. Because we're all friends."

Vyll looked up again. This time, he looked like he was close to tears, even though Kara was pretty sure that Protectors couldn't cry. "This is the best gift anyone has ever given me. Though I guess that isn't saying much; this is my very first gift, after all."

"'The first of many,' as Master Hoyan always says," said Carem. He nodded at Vyll. "I got a gift for you, too, but it's too big for me to carry around in my pockets. I was planning to give it to you tomorrow, for your birthday, but since sis here gave you yours now, I guess I can go ahead and give it to you when we get back to the house."

Vyll's mouth fell open. "That would be … my second gift. That means I will have two gifts, even though up until now I have not even had one."

"I know!" said Kara. "Isn't that amazing? I mean, I don't really understand it all that well, because I've always gotten a gift every year for my birthday, but I'm happy that you're happy."

"Happy?" said Vyll. He held the picture closer to his chest.

8

"Yes, I guess you could say I am happy. Is this what happiness is like? All of us being together like this?"

"Sure," said Kara. A warm breeze her hair around a little, but she ignored it. "Everyone's happier when they're together with friends or family. I know I'm always happy whenever my parents, Carem, you, and I are together."

"Happiness is … togetherness, then," said Vyll. "I will remember that always, Kara. That, and this gift you gave me."

Kara's smile widened even more. "That makes *me* happy."

Vyll looked at Carem. "What about you, Carem? Does that make you happy as well?"

"Sure," said Carem, jamming his hands into his pockets. "But I'll be even happier when you see the gift I got ya. It's way better than a funny little drawing."

Kara scowled at Carem. "Funny little drawing? It took me *hours* to get the colors right. I worked hard on it and even included you on it."

Carem smirked and held up his hands. "Doesn't change the fact that it's not all that great. I bet I could draw a better picture with both arms tied behind my back and Master Hoyan yelling in my ears."

"Oh, yeah?" said Kara. She pointed at the house in the distance. "Then why don't we have a drawing contest when we get home? Whoever draws the better picture wins."

Vyll stepped forward. His red optics looked concerned and he clutched the picture tighter than ever. "Why are you two going to fight? I thought we were all together."

"Fight? It's not a fight," said Carem. "Just a contest to see who's better, that's all."

"Oh," said Vyll. He stroked his chin. "Contest ... yes, I think I recall hearing that word before. You have entered sword contests before, right, Master Carem?"

"Right," said Carem, nodding. He jabbed his thumb at his chest. "Only a few so far, though, but I came in second place in the last one. Only reason I didn't win is because that kid from Jaggen used a dirty trick."

"You lost fair and square," Kara pointed out. "He didn't use any dirty trick. You just aren't as good as you think you are, that's all."

"Whatever, Kara," said Carem, rolling his eyes. "Anyway, let's go home and start that contest. If we're fast, we might be able to do it before we head into the city for the celebration. See you there!"

Carem took off through the tall grass, heading directly to the house. Kara followed as fast as she could, already forgetting about that giant monster snake that Vyll had killed. She was now more concerned with beating her older brother to house, because she knew that if she didn't get there first, he'd gloat about winning the race all day long even if he ended up losing the picture-drawing contest.

Even so, she glanced over her shoulder at Vyll. He had not followed them yet; instead, he was still staring at the picture like it was the most valuable treasure in the world.

Although Kara hated to let Carem get any further ahead of her than he already was, she stopped for a moment and shouted, "Vyll! Are you coming or not? Remember, Carem's got a gift for you back home that he wants to give you!"

Vyll shook his head and looked at her. He raise a hand and

shouted back, "I'm coming, Kara. Just give me a moment to catch up. You can go on ahead with Carem."

Kara frowned. "But—"

"Carem is going to win the race if you stay here," said Vyll. "Remember?"

Kara still wanted to make sure Vyll was coming (because she was now starting to remember the snake again and worried that there might be more hiding nearby that might harm Vyll), but then she decided that Vyll was more capable of defending himself than most adults were.

So she nodded and replied, "All right! See you later, then. Just get back before we start the contest; we need a judge and you're the best judge I know."

With that, Kara turned and resumed running after her brother. He was quite a ways ahead of her now, but Kara was certain that she would catch up with him well before they reached the house.

Even so, she could not help but look back at Vyll every now and then until he was lost from sight within the tall, scratchy grass. She was just glad that he liked her drawing. It made her so happy that she doubted even Carem winning the race or the drawing contest would be enough to put her in a bad mood for the rest of the day.

We'll be together forever, Kara thought as she ran. *Me, Carem, and Vyll. Even when we grow up, we'll still be tied together. Just like we promised.*

-

Desinence is now available in ebook and trade paperback wherever books are sold!

About the Author

Timothy L. Cerepaka writes fantasy and science-fiction stories as an indie author. He is the author of the Prince Malock World fantasy novels, the Mages of Martir fantasy novels, and the science-fantasy standalone *The Last Legend: Glitch Apocalypse*. He lives in Texas.

Go to his website at www.timothylcerepaka.com to find out more.

Other books by Timothy L. Cerepaka

Prince Malock World:

The Mad Voyage of Prince Malock

The Return of Prince Malock

The New Era of Prince Malock

The Coronation of Prince Malock

Mages of Martir:

The Mage's Grave

The Mage's Limits

The Mage's Sea

The Mage's Ghost

Two Worlds:

Reunification

Alliance

Allegiance

Retaliation

Desinence

Standalones:

The Last Legend: Glitch Apocalypse

All of the above books are available in ebook and trade paperback wherever books are sold!

www.ingramcontent.com/pod-product-compliance
Lightning Source LLC
Chambersburg PA
CBHW061206170626
46809CB00003B/1259